Praise for The Film You Are About to See

"Buttery snack bar popcorn, drive-in intermission ads, classic horror cinephilia: clearly I'm the target audience for this book. But I think you'll love it too. *The Film You Are About to See* is a book with its eyes on the past, but at the same time announces Newlin as a modern horror voice to watch.
"It's showtime!"
—Adam Cesare, Bram-Stoker-Award©-winning author of *Clown In a Cornfield*

"The book you are about to read is a cinephile's spine-tingling fever dream. Haley Newlin pens a love letter to celluloid, capturing the grain and gimmicks of a bygone era where the blood seeps right off the screen and into your book. William Castle would be proud... and you'll be absolutely terrified."
—Clay McLeod Chapman, author of *Wake Up and Open Your Eyes*

"Retro, raucous, and a roaring good time, *The Film You Are About to See* is a must-read for horror fans everywhere. An absolute blood-soaked delight."
—Gwendolyn Kiste, four-time Bram-Stoker-Award©-winning author of *Reluctant Immortals*

"Energetic and full of popcorn and bodies. The Film You Are About to See pays loving tribute to the classic horror of yesteryear with a blood-soaked romp at the drive-in."
—Hailey Piper, author of *A Light Most Hateful*

"Newlin takes everything we love about classic horror films and the drive-in experience, turning pages into silver screens with piercing screams."
—**Nick Roberts, author of *Mean Spirited* and *The Exorcist's House***

"Like a mad scientist from the films of yore, Haley Newlin has crafted a delightfully deranged spectacle on the page with *The Film You Are About to See*. You'll never want to leave this blood-soaked drive-in... but the creepy thing in your backseat won't let you anyway."
—**Brian McAuley, author of *Breathe In, Bleed Out* and *Curse of the Reaper***

"*The Film You Are About to See* is a spooktastic tribute to classic horror films that will leave your spine tingling. With a kick ass heroine, gore galore, and the creepiest creature ever to grace a drive-in, you'll devour this novella faster than a bucket of movie theater popcorn!"
—**Angela Sylvaine, Bram-Stoker-Award©-nominated author of *Frost Bite* and *Chopping Spree***

"A terrifying love letter to the drive-in movie era where the real creature feature is off-screen. The perfect bloody homage to William Castle and Vincent Price horror."
—**Wendy Dalrymple, author of *Credenza* and *Birthday Party Demon***

"*The Film You Are About to See* has all the glorious flavor of a classic horror movie combined with characters you can't help but love. Haley Newlin's writing evokes both a 1950s time capsule and a fun, monster-filled romp you won't be able to put down."

—Viggy Parr Hampton, author of *The Rotting Room*

"From the opening reel to the final frame, *The Film You Are About to See* is bursting with monster-movie mayhem. This is drive-in horror at its gleefully bloody, devilishly fun, and heart-felt best!"

—V.S. Lawrence, author of *80s Ghosts* and *With Friends Like These*

"Full of appreciation for the genre, beautifully written, and above all, a really fun time, wrapped in a celluloid skin of pure retro camp, *The Film You Are About to See* is a story that will not release readers from its pincered grip until the end credits roll. With nods to Castle and Price and their B-Movie brethren, this is a creature feature with claws and brains that is not to be missed."

—FanFiAddict

HALEY NEWLIN

MADAXEMEDIA.COM

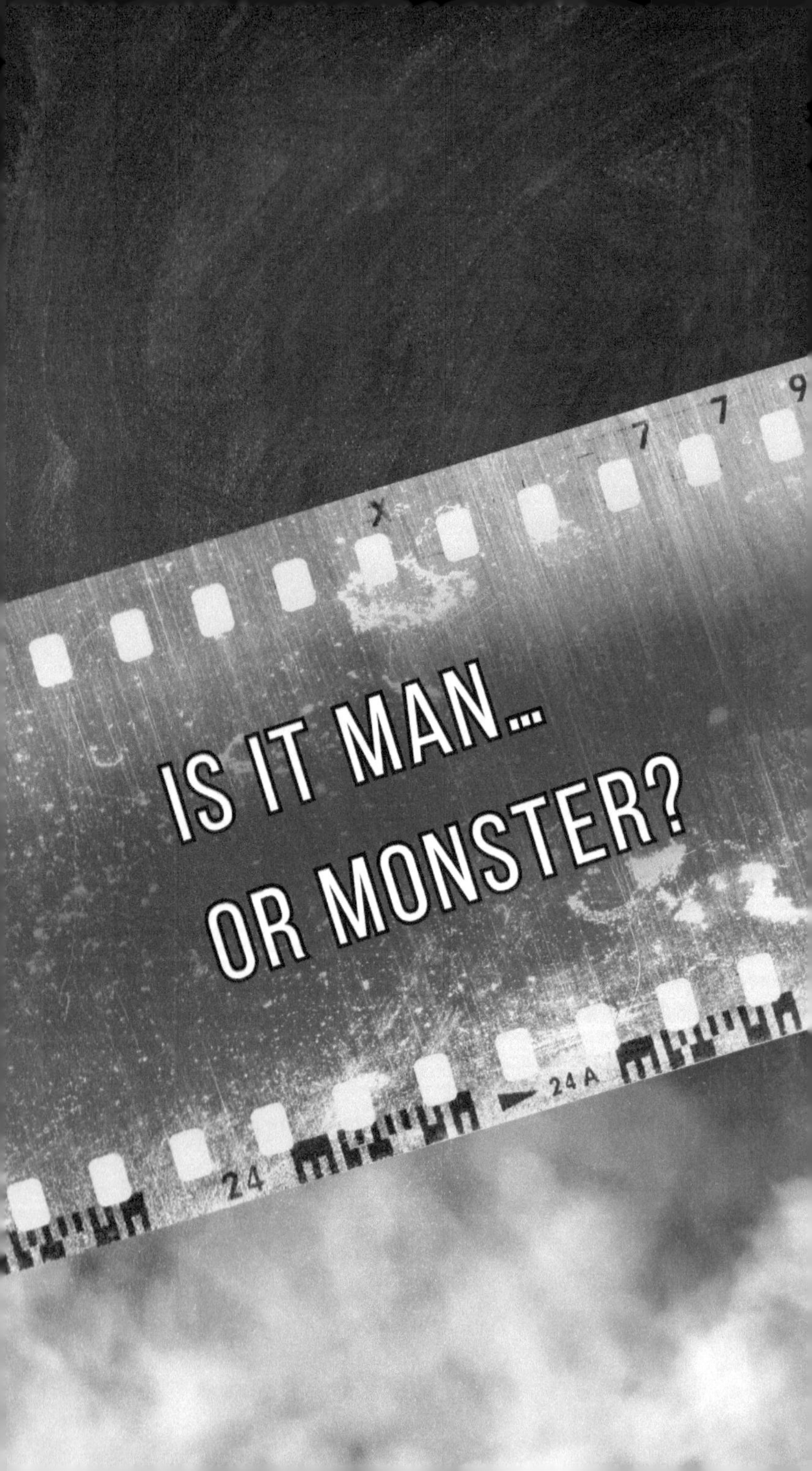

IS IT MAN...
OR MONSTER?

THE ANSWER MAY BE
TOO TERRIFYING
TO KNOW!

Published by Mad Axe Media

Cover & Interior Design by Joey Powell

Edited by Clayton Bohle

Print ISBN: 978-1-966497-10-3

E-Book ISBN: 978-1-966497-11-0

For the two who started it all, William Castle and Vincent Price

"I'm going to give the people what they want. Sensation. Horror. Shock. Send them out in the streets to tell their friends how wonderful it is to be scared to death."
—Vincent Price as Professor Henry Jarrod in *House of Wax* (1953)

The Film You are About To See

AN INTRODUCTION
FROM THE AUTHOR

"And remember this, a scream at the right time, may save your life." – William Castle, The Tingler

When I was six years old, I came home from school and found my mother's car in the drive. Surprised and excited to see her home an hour or so early, I hurried into the house, my identical twin sister on my heels. My mother wasn't in the living room, so we checked her bedroom where she often paced, munching on chips and salsa, and chatting on the home phone with a friend from down the street.

She wasn't there either. The adjoined master bathroom door yawned open.

"Mom?" We called in unison, to our annoyance, as we often did.

No answer.

We inched closer, exchanging quick glances.

"Mom?" My sister tried again. I raised a hand, stopping her. I pointed to the white tile floor inside. It was spotted with brilliant red.

I pushed the bathroom door wide and into the wall and gasped. The bathtub was stained red, too, only a few shades deeper. With no explanation of the source for this logic, I thought that meant this blood had been there longer. Had Mom hurt herself somehow in the tub, stumbled out, and dripped fresh rivulets across the bleach-treated tile? If so, how long had she been hurt? Was she alright?

There's some disagreement about who cried first, me or my sister, but I'd wager we both gave in to distress. "Mom?" We tried once more.

"Dammit," my mother's voice came from the hall. "Dog spends its whole life outside, sees all kinds of wild animals, but when it catches a glimpse of the housecat it goes insane."

She exhaled, exasperated. "Yes, Trace, I know it was the cat who bit me, but the dog terrified her."

She came into the room with the phone held between her ear and shoulder. She wrapped a dish towel around her palm.

"Katie bit you?" my sister asked. Katie was our German Shepherd.

It took my mom a moment to clock our tears, the pain of her bloodied hand clouding her otherwise precise suspicions.

"It was Carly," I said. Carly was our cat.

Our eyes went to the tub and then back to our mother's wet hair. Globs of crimson hair color stained her forehead and around her ears. She never had the patience to do it with a dye brush and gloves.

That explained the color of the tub. Mom got off early, came home and colored her hair, rinsed it, and did laundry. When she'd opened the backdoor to hang sheets on the line outside, the German Shepherd spotted the cat, who my mom had been holding at the time, and growled ferociously. Startled, the cat sank its teeth into my mother's hand and clawed herself free.

My sister went about her night, telling stories at dinner, but I had a bit more trouble letting go of the horror I'd felt coming home from school that day, wondering if something awful had happened. At this ridiculously young age, I began to wonder what life would be like without someone I loved around. Even worse, if I saw how they left. If I found them bloodied in the bathtub or their lifeless body spilled on the bathroom floor.

I had nightmares for weeks.

Years later, I stayed with my grandfather for a chunk of the summer as my mother finalized a particularly difficult divorce. Leaving her alone in the house triggered an assortment of fears for her safety. Ours, too.

After dinner one night, my grandfather retired to bed early, and my mind raced.

Apparently, my sister's mind did too, as she sat up and declared, "I can't sleep."

We turned on the old TV that stood on four short legs and within a golden frame that curled like Greek architecture.

None of our usual channels promised any good watches. In fact, it was close to Halloween and though my sister didn't like to admit it, she didn't like watching Halloween specials at night, especially if I fell asleep first.

Remote in hand and being a full thirty minutes older, I chose a title I recognized: *Psycho*. I'd never seen the film before but had seen a few episodes of *Alfred Hitchcock Presents*. And though *Psycho* was labeled as a horror title, it was in black and white and, therefore, mild, even tame, I'd assumed.

But the television program ran behind. *Psycho* wouldn't play for another forty-five minutes. Instead, on screen, was a man in a director's chair, film equipment framing him in the shot. "Hello, my name is William Castle. I feel obligated to warn you about . . . *The Tingler.*"

Castle promised that filmgoers would actually play a part in the action on screen while in the theatre. I wondered how I would do so, immediately transported into a theatre audience at one of the first showings of *The Tingler* in 1959. Castle promised more shocks per minute in this film than his previous release, *House On Haunted Hill*. The screen cut into a film trailer unlike any I'd ever seen. Floating heads emerged on screen, screaming shrill, unnerving shrieks.

"Turn it down," my sister whisper-shouted, clearly disturbed.

I fumbled for the volume button and quieted the screams that admittedly gave me quite the fright, too. I was also afraid of waking my grandfather and his wife. Of being bad house guests and being sent home.

TCM appeared in the bottom corner of the screen and a man laughed to himself, going on about the legendary William Castle and his gimmicks.

Then, he said, "And now back to the film."

A woman named Mrs. Martha Ryerson Higgins, played by Judith Evelyn, awoke from sedation to a series of horrors. A hairy arm reached from dreadfully slow opening doors, holding a hatchet just inches above her head. Her eyes widened in shock, but she didn't scream. A bathroom door opened, seemingly on its own. Mrs. Higgins stumbled inside, and the same look of terror poured over her face. The faucet, in this otherwise black and white movie, was spewing brilliant, bright red blood. And not just in the sink, but the bathtub, too.

I turned to my sister, "Do you remember that day after school?"

I didn't have to repaint the image of Mom's bloody hand or the "blood-spotted" tile or the stained tub. Twin thing, I suppose.

My sister nodded as we watched a blood-soaked hand reach from the tub on screen.

"We were so scared," I said. I remember wanting to scream then.

"Why isn't she screaming?" I said of Mrs. Higgins.

My sister shook her head. She didn't understand it either.

We had to know.

We watched the rest of the film, and learned that Mrs. Higgins was a non-hearing, non-verbal woman who couldn't release her scream, and therefore couldn't dispel the creature that grows upon every human's spine as fear mounds within them. Studying this phenomenon was a pathologist, played by the infamous Vincent Price, who of course we were drawn to right away.

We loved *The Tingler*, and I ran into my grandfather's kitchen, hunting for something to write down the film title as well as the one William Castle mentioned during TCM's replay of the old trailer for *The Tingler*. *House On Haunted Hill*, it was called.

TCM showed that one, too, just a few days later. And we learned that Price starred in this film as well, and that *The Tingler* wasn't the first film where Castle employed his iconic gimmicks.

We had so much fun watching these films for the first time. And with TCM's incredible commentary, Castle's devious and juvenile showmanship, and Price's charm, we were hooked.

And, we were able to suspend enough disbelief, sidestep the occasional goof like a hard-to-miss wire pulling a creature along its way, to imagine what it would've been like to see these films in-univertheatre when they'd first debuted. This made them all the more terrifying. And of course, all the more fun.

I hung on to these movies for years to come, diving headfirst into the horror genre, remembering how I'd felt that day I came home from school, the red hair color, and of course, how *The Tingler* took me back to that place years later.

That's how good horror works, I thought.

For this and all the reasons above, I've written *The Film You Are About To See*. I imagined giving modern horror fans, friends, and family the experience of oldies horror films, especially those produced or directed by William Castle and starring Vincent Price. And watching horror movies from the 50s and early 60s, of course, introduced me to car culture and, therefore, the horror drive-in experience. This would be where I'd discover Universal monster pictures like *Dracula* and other horror classics such as *The Blob*.

When you stumble on the marquee in *The Film You Are About To See,* you may be surprised to see that I did not select a single Universal monster flick.

GASP!

The audacity, right?

I juggled with that decision, but my editor, Clay, *pause for applause*, reminded me that this idea stemmed from what I imagined I would show if I got to host a DUSK TIL DAWN horror show at the local drive-in. Better yet, if I could somehow recreate Castle's famous gimmicks like *Emergo!* where a skeleton flew over the heads of theatre goers during a showing of *House On Haunted Hill*. Or *Percepto!* where Castle and his crew stationed vibrating devices underneath theatre seats during showings of *The Tingler*.

And that conjured the idea, rather the fascination, of this momentary terror where the line between theatrics and real-life horror blurred.

And so, that's what I hope to bring you in *The Film You Are About To See*. An experience that hasn't been captured quite as effectively since the 1950s, a limbo of pranks and terror. The urge to scream while everyone else laughs as if they were all in on it all along.

Please note, to bring you the oldies horror experience as I had it, I employ a few tricks outside of their timeline. For example, I couldn't leave out one of Castle's 1961 gimmicks that always cracked me up called "The Fright Break." For The Fright Break, Castle interrupts the film and offers a chance for anyone too afraid to finish the movie to exit the theatre. However, if you did, Castle encouraged the audience to taunt you, to point and laugh at anyone heading for what he called "The Coward's Corner."

You'll also note a playful spelling of the school mascot. This is intentional and a nod to my alma-mater. And it's actually a completely accepted spelling of the word, no matter what Mike Salt tells you.

So, grab some popcorn, lean in close, because *The Film You Are About To See* is one I hope you carry with you for years to come, just as I have these oldies titles I hold so near and dear. For those of you who've enjoyed these films just as I have, I hope this book reminds you of times both pleasant and not so much, because after all, horror, like life, is a constant limbo. And of course, I hope I get you with a few scares of my own. This is a love letter to oldies horror, but it's still a horror story of its own, and as Vincent Price says in *Haunted Palace* (1963, directed by Roger Corman), "I'm entitled to a few amusements."

Thanks for going on this journey with me. I hope I make oldies horror fans of you all.

Yours (Horrifically),
Haley Newlin

P.S. Keep a pen nearby. Every film mentioned in this book, on the marquee or otherwise, comes with a LOUD, SCREAM-ING, BLEEDING stamp of approval from me.

CHAPTER ONE

It's alive!

Thursday, August 6, 1959

8:30 PM

An impending storm bruised the evening sky a corpse-blue and purple. Wild wind blasted through the night. Trees bent against the force. Carrion beetles, or "burying bugs," as some referred to them, skittered from tree roots and across the forest floor. Birds squawked overhead, distressed and in search of sanctuary in the expanse of soaring oak trees. The rain came down heavy and fast and all at once. Ominous flashes of lightning reached from the clouds and clear to the ground. Steam rose from the undergrowth as the muggy air cooled.

As the electric shocks across the dark sky grew more frequent, a single strike broke away and zapped straight through the tallest cherrybark oak tree standing. Bark burst as the current singed through the tree, limbs to its buried roots, with a *hiss*.

Its fall awakened something underground. A long forgotten, cursed creature.

Born in steam, it unfurled like smoke. It was without immediate recollection of its purpose. It came with a bare consciousness, a sponge ready to absorb matter. But then, it began to remember things. Pain and fear. Life and death. To hunt and to be hunted. Humans. Which drew forth a single word. *Monsters.*

They were one in the same, the creature remembered.

Rain slashed through the swirling mist as it detached from the natural plumes. It could feel the great power of the storm surging through it, and it wanted to test its strength.

It sensed a warmth it knew to be an indication of living organisms, and it was approaching.

Monsters.

It wanted to feed upon them. This violent desire was evolutionary, and the creature's smokey substance transformed. It solidified as limbs shot from its sides with wet and slick snaps, and two long, clicking pincers grew from its head.

The creature dropped to the earth's floor. It thrashed against the landscape, adjusting to its form as the humans approached. When they neared, the creature steadied itself on its spindly legs and scurried to the fallen limbs for cover. There, as carrion beetles hurried beside it, the creature waited.

Through the thinning rain, the creature saw two orbs of light bob closer. Into the clearing, littered with chips of bark and fallen branches, stepped a young man in light wash jeans, cuffs rolled, and a tucked white t-shirt. His mouth fell open as he gaped at the natural wreckage before him. As his light wandered along the fallen oak, it passed over the creature. It pressed itself lower against the ground, still as death.

"Jim, come see this!" His eyes were wide in disbelief. "Man, this one got done in! You could hear it all the way from concessions."

A slightly older boy, thinner than the other, with tightly combed hair and a slim mustache, stopped in the clearing. His own light spread in tight rays across the forest and up the towering trees. He frowned.

"Ralph, you know how hard it is to take down an oak tree?"

Ralph was still scratching his head. "Man, I wonder if I heard the lightning strike, the tree split, or what?"

Ralph sliced his hand, as if it was the sharp blade of an axe, toward the log.

"Wait a minute." His eyes widened. "I know what this is. It's the healing tree. It's like 400 years old," Ralph said.

Ralph crouched down to inspect the scarred tree.

"My folks call it the hanging tree," Jim said. "They say unmarked graves lie beneath each oak out here."

"What? No," Ralph protested, perhaps a little afraid. "It's not a ghost story. It's a wishing well. People come and offer a piece of cloth, tie it to a branch, and ask the healing gods for help. "

Jim pointed the light over his shoulder, assessing the trees behind him, then to his side, then back to the fallen oak.

"I've heard that one, too. I heard another story about a witch." Jim huffed.

This was the creature's chance. It crept through the brush and debris and onto Jim's muddied shoes. It crawled up his pant leg, and as the man squirmed, the creature followed a rush of delicious panicked energy up Jim's bony spine to his brain stem. Jim screamed just as the creature's pincers dug in.

Ralph screamed in response and fell away from the tree and onto his palms, his pants soiled in mud.

Angered hardened Ralph's face.

"Dammit, Jim! These are my good slacks. Save it for the Spooktacular tomorrow."

Jim didn't reply. He couldn't. The creature wouldn't let him. Jim's body straightened up, a soldier in salute, awaiting command.

"Jim?"

Distant echoes of thunder clapped. Ralph jolted in surprise and brought a hand to his startled heart as he rose to his feet.

"Jim? You alright?"

For the creature, Jim's fear was palpable and so gloriously warm. It clicked its pincers and raised all of its legs at once, like a pair of wings, then clamped down, tightening around its host's spine. Jim stepped forward.

Fear quaked through each word as Ralph said, "Hey, let's just head back to rehearsal."

The creature was on fire with pleasure, the thrill of terrifying this human and its host, too. In Jim's skin, the creature approached a confused Ralph, who put his hands up in defense.

"Jim?" Ralph said, taking a step back.

He turned to run, and the creature caught Ralph by the shoulder. It squeezed, feeling its host's fingers dig into the man's flesh. Ralph shouted in pain, and the creature forced him to his knees with ease. Ralph crumbled, whimpering.

"Jim, what are you doing?"

Ralph groaned and wiggled against the stronghold.

"Jim, let go."

Jim's brain remained active and alive, but the creature wouldn't allow him to form any words. Not to be spoken aloud, anyway. His breath came out in quick succession. Sweat poured down his face. He reeked of perspiration and piss. Of terror.

The creature guided his host's free hand toward the man's face. Ralph followed the movement with wide eyes, still struggling against the creature's grasp.

"Jim!" Ralph shrieked. His eyes were bright with horror. Desperation. They flitted left, then right, perhaps searching for any sign of life. "Help!" he screamed, but the creature knew they were alone.

The creature seized a handful of Ralph's gel-slick hair and yanked him in front of the fallen tree.

"Jim, stop!"

With a force Jim had never possessed before, he slammed Ralph's skull against the oak's stump. It wasn't him, though. It was the creature. A wail escaped his mouth as the creature made him reel Ralph's head back and down again. Blood exploded from Ralph's nose that sat fractured and askew. His lips were smashed.

"Je-hem!" he sobbed, pleading through the swelling.

Jim's bewildered eyes were glassy with tears. He couldn't stop himself, and, oh, how that delighted the creature all the more.

Once more, the creature brought Ralph's head back. Only this time it held the boy like this for just a moment. Just long enough for his eyes to meet Jim's.

What have I done? Jim thought.

Then, he gritted his teeth, the furious strength fuming inside him and the next collision between face and tree silenced Ralph. His body fell from the tree, face obliterated. Beyond recognition.

The creature forced Jim to lower himself to his knees, before the oak tree and his bludgeoned fellow actor.

The creature felt Jim quiver as he placed his hands atop the scarred tree. He wept as he brought his head back, base to spine, then down, *hard* onto the wood. A few of his teeth shattered, and his head struck the tree once more before he could spit them out. He swallowed them.

By the third impact, his face was annihilated. Strings of reds and white fell from his face. A cheekbone exposed and splintered into a fracture. His nose shoved too far to the left.

The heat melted away, and the creature detached from the man's spine.

It felt renewed. Restored. But it needed more. Lots more.

It left behind the oak tree from whence it came and the two mangled men. It pressed onward through the woods. Toward the warmth of other humans just through the break in the woods.

An enormous shadow loomed over it. On the other side was a bright box of light with moving pictures of humans running from a building, a gelatinous and all-consuming blob behind them.

A contraption made of metal with curtained windows sat below the screen. The creature lay in wait as a brooding, beastly man stomped across the clearing, carrying something covered in a sheet. A body, the creature realized.

"Makin' me set this crap up in the dang mud," the man complained. He dumped the body beside the—the word came to it, from that little bit of consciousness it had slurped up from the thin man—*vehicle*.

In the small building a ways back came a crash, the unmistakable sound of shattered glass. "Good grief," the man said. "Now what?"

He adjusted the sheet haphazardly and the body fell flat. He exhaled an angry grunt and was done with the thing.

"Hell with it."

He stomped toward the ruckus.

The creature moved quickly. It ducked under the sheet. It thought the thin man had been frail, but it could feel every bumpy knot of bone on this host's spine. It nestled into position and gripped the spine with its spindly legs and curled, and the person sat up from beneath the sheet. The creature clicked its pincers before sending them into the person's neck.

But it didn't take.

It clicked its pincers in frustration and tried once more.

There was no immediate warmth.

This human had no skin. No thoughts or fears.

It flitted up and down the body. This human wasn't human at all. It was an imitation. All bones and no flesh.

A skeleton.

It wasn't deterred, for the man who dumped the skeleton had been summoned away by other humans. And it could feel them. They were so warm.

The creature wriggled ahead.

Monday, August 3, 1959
8:30 AM

G rey clouds loomed over the town like an impending curse.

"You think the drive-in will get rained out Friday?" June asked her friends Ingrid and Stef as they jogged around their high school's dirt track. Dust swirled at their feet. She remembered the goofy weatherman from the night before, warning of violent thunderstorms. The forecasts were only 48 hours ahead, but in August—especially in Indiana—when the hot and cold air intermingled, storms rumbled throughout the town for as long as a week at a time. And the drive-in lot was a glorified, short-trimmed lawn with dirt paths.

"Get outta here," Stef said. "They can't cancel the first-ever DUSK TIL DAWN SPOOKTACULAR." She raised her hand, imitating Bela Lugosi when enchanting, or cursing, a poor soul.

June giggled, finding it hilarious that her friend referenced a movie she was only able to steal a few glances of. She'd spent the rest of the film covering her eyes. When June had stayed at Stef's that night years ago, Stef woke her each time she had to use the restroom and made June stand in the bath with the shower curtain closed. Then, June had to lead the way back down the dark hall to Stef's room.

Stef's ponytail bounced as she jogged. Her red hair, which came from her mother, an Irish immigrant, was radiant and bright even on that gloomy day.

"My grandpa said the rain is here to stay," Ingrid chimed in. Ingrid's black bangs blew on either side of her face.

"Oh yeah? What does he know?" Stef teased.

The rest of Ingrid's short hair was flounced and curled. Ingrid was always careful not to exert too much energy in P.E. class. It was a lot of work to keep those curls spun just so, and she didn't want to ruin her hair. She walked just fast enough to keep Miss Desjardin off her back. June understood, as she meticulously styled her own blonde bangs each morning, curling them tight in a single roll across the width of her forehead.

Ingrid also despised how different the girls' activities were from the boys'.

Ingrid gave Stef a shove. "He's usually right about these things. Says he can feel it in his bones."

"Spooooky," Stef said, drawing the word out ghoulishly.

"Yeah," Ingrid said. "It's scary getting old."

June hoped they didn't cancel the DUSK TIL DAWN SPOOKTACULAR at Peterson's Pictures Drive-In. She'd seen all her favorite horror movies there: *Dracula*, *Creature From The Black Lagoon*, *Invasion of the Body Snatchers*, *The Blob*, and just about every film Vincent Price had ever starred in. She couldn't wait to see what they loaded the marquee with for the Friday special.

Just then, June felt something over her shoulder. Not eyes. She never had that "somebody's watching me" feeling. It was more like *she* should be watching . . . paying attention. Something was going to happen. Something bad.

She looked for a sign. Spinning herself around, panting.

A cluster of girls sped by them in their red-collared P.E. uniforms, startling June. The girl at the front, Annie, scoffed at June. "She's such a fraidy cat." The others laughed.

"Fraidy Cat. Fraidy Cat," the girls teased.

It wasn't hard to summon June's shame, and it found her instantly. She crossed her arms, trying to let it roll off of her.

This taunt was nothing new. June had had more than a few incidents throughout the years, at slumber parties, basketball games, classrooms, and even on the playground in elementary school. These sudden shocks of pain or nerves that vibrated down her spine and throbbed inside her skull. Sometimes she'd daze out. Other times, the pain was so awful, she'd sob or even scream. Those were the worst. And every now and then, if she let the sense linger too long, she'd be carried off to scenes of death, sometimes hundreds of miles away.

"Stuff it," Ingrid retorted. She glanced over and saw Miss Desjardin occupied with the cheerleaders. So she tucked her hand down her top and retrieved a matchbook from her bra. She tucked a cigarette between her lips and lit it.

Annie glowered at Ingrid.

"You know, I could tell on you for smoking in class."

"You could," Ingrid said.

Annie's friends smirked, thinking they'd won.

Ingrid took a drag of her cigarette and doused the opposing girl with smoke. "And I could tell your mother that I saw you skinny dipping in the ravine."

The girls behind Annie gasped.

Before Annie could say another word, Ingrid continued, "Oh, and with a boy!"

Annie's friends exchanged shocked glances. A few of their faces soured, wounded by their friend's secrecy.

There it was again, that nagging tug. Something June needed to pick up on but couldn't quite dial into. Her heart fluttered in her chest. She cracked her knuckles, growing more anxious by the second.

"And not just any boy. The pastor's son," Ingrid added.

Annie's friends were bouncing on their heels, squealing and gasping.

"Pipe down!" Annie shouted at them, stomping her feet in the dirt. Then she turned to Ingrid with stone cold anger in her dark blue eyes.

"You wouldn't dare," Annie punched each word so it landed as a threat.

Ingrid's bright red lips curved into a satisfied grin. "Absolutely, I would."

"That ought to dampen your weekend plans," Stef said.

Annie's face flushed with embarrassment. Her friends whispered amongst themselves about the newfound knowledge of her nude rendezvous with the pastor's son and lowerclassman, William.

"Zip it!" Annie ordered the group. She jogged away, the others following behind.

Stef cackled. "Is that true? About her and William?"

Ingrid blew smoke from pursed lips. "Saw it myself."

"And you didn't tell us?!" Stef said, shoving Ingrid.

Orange embers fell from Ingrid's cigarette.

Miss Desjardin blew her whistle, signaling to the cheerleaders on the other side of the track. June turned her attention to them and felt as if she'd swallowed a stone. It sat in her throat, a dry lump cutting off her breath. It sank to her stomach, sitting heavy like a meal eaten much too quickly.

The cheerleaders leapt and tossed their red and white pom poms. "B-R-O-N-C-H-O-S!" they chanted. "B-R-O-N-C-H-O-S!"

June lowered her head. It suddenly weighed a ton. Even with a heavy overcast, the daylight worsened the pain. She covered her face.

"Oh, June. Don't let Annie get to you," Stef consoled her. "She's just a snob."

Ingrid blew smoke away from June and then patted her back.

"Let's talk about Friday's show," Ingrid encouraged.

She always tried to steer things right for the gang.

"So, we'll take the Studebaker, and Vincent can drive the boys in the truck," Ingrid said. "Right, June?"

June tried to refocus. Ignore the trigger. But she couldn't break her gaze from the cheerleaders.

"Earth to June," Stef said, waving her arms, but June was transfixed, and her friend might as well have been on another planet.

Janice, a petite cheerleader, leapt high in the air, touching her toes.

Miss Desjardin blew the whistle and the girls got back in formation.

"Bronchos!" The squad chanted in unison. "B-R-O-N-C-H-O-S!"

This time, when Janice swung her arms and jumped into the air to repeat the toe-touch, she leaned hard to the right. Panic burned in June's chest.

Janice landed awkwardly and rolled off one ankle. She crashed to the ground with a loud cry.

Ingrid and Stef recoiled.

"Oh my gosh," Stef said.

June felt the hot pain of her own ankle break. But she flexed her leg muscles and held herself up. It would pass. No matter how long the pain sat with her, it always passed.

Janice would be okay, June reasoned. Sure, a broken ankle is painful, but it could be mended. That didn't satisfy the dread within.

"I think she broke it," Ingrid offered as Janice tested pressure on the foot and reintroduced the pain to herself and June.

June winced.

Janice beckoned for her squad members, who helped her to her feet. Two cheerleaders served as crutches as they made for the nurse's office on the other side of the school.

"She did," June said, still fighting the pain.

Thunder rumbled in the distance, and June knew that there was more her sense was trying to tell her. Every nerve in her body yelled at her at once, but they were speaking another language. Sometimes the sense was a riddle she couldn't decipher.

June spun around. "Something is happening."

Run.

Run where? she thought.

"June, what's going on?" Ingrid asked. She flicked her cigarette into a small puddle.

A part of June detached from her physical form. She blinked and was somewhere else. Outside her grandmother's home. She'd recognize the blood red door anywhere. Since her grandmother had stopped attending church, the neighbors said she'd invited Satan in through her devil door.

A black-gloved hand, too big to be her own, pushed the door open. The living room was dim, a mess of shadows in the gloomy light peaking through the worn curtains. A shadow stretched across the bright flooring. It wasn't hers. This figure was much broader than her. Its frame muscular and massive.

The coffee table's drawers flew open. The gloved hands rifled through the drawers, tossing aside family photos, her grandmother's stationary, and a pack of cigarettes.

The cabinet doors where her grandmother kept her vinyl records flew open. Behind a front facing record, Billy Holiday's *At Jazz At The Philharmonic,* was a large rinsed tomato soup can, full of cash and coins. Her grandmother kept several cans like this hidden around the house. She said she didn't trust the banks.

Framed photos toppled from shelves and crashed to the floor as the intruder searched the house further.

Swish, swish, swish.

The sound of her grandmother's slippers against the hard floor came down the hall and into the living room. June turned and saw her grandmother, but the perspective was all wrong. June was too tall. June saw fear and anger play across her grandmother's face.

She swung at June and screamed, "Get out! Get out before I call the police!"

Grandma it's me, June thought, but the words wouldn't materialize and June knew this wasn't truly her. She was watching through the eyes of someone else.

This intruder approached her grandmother, taking every hit that June felt at the center of her chest. Her grandmother backed into her wallpapered bedroom. Behind her was her bed and a wooden nightstand.

Run.

"Just tell me where the rest of the cash is, and then I'm gone," came a man's voice. It was as if he was standing on top of June, or she was on top of him. It was happening again.

"Get out!" her grandmother shouted at the intruder.

Her grandmother continued to beat the intruder and it hurt too bad for her to be proud of her grandmother's efforts. She certainly packed a mightier punch than one would suspect. June watched from his perspective as the intruder grabbed her grandmother's wrists, restraining her. Her grandmother tossed her knee into the side of his leg, and he answered with a powerful shove.

In the momentum of her grandmother's fall, June snapped back to herself and she stumbled. A sharp pain blossomed across the back of her head.

"June? What's the matter?" a voice said, though she was too out of it to distinguish whether it was Ingrid or Stef.

Run.

She knew how this was going to end. Otherwise, she wouldn't be seeing it. When she saw pain like this, fear too, it only meant one thing.

Death.

But she was going to beat it. She had to.

She ran.

Thunder applauded the distress like an audience, and rain fell violently as she crossed the school yard and to the intersection at Kossuth and Earl Avenue. The precipitation soaked through her scratchy starch shorts and the matching top. Her hair crumpled around her face like a wet rag.

She blazed by the old pharmacy and soda shop. Its awning flapped in the wind. She jumped an enormous puddle clotting outside the storm drain.

Her sneakers stomped through small pools of dingy water and showered her calves and ankles.

She hurried through a neighboring area of young families with new babies. Then, she crossed a few lawns, one abandoned and overgrown, and to her street. She ran past the driveways, all with cars parked in them, from trucks to Chevys and Cadillacs.

She lunged up the drive to her house and threw the front door open.

"Mom," June hollered. The vinyl furniture was empty. Though there were fresh impressions on the carpet from the vacuum cleaner.

June hurried into the kitchen. A tea kettle sat atop the stove. But her mother wasn't there.

"Mom," she cried, tears rushing her all at once. "Mom!"

She tore through the house, checking her parents' bedroom, then her own bedroom, where her mother did her sewing because she said it was the room with the best source of natural light. On her dresser sat her mother's pin cushion, bright silver stabbed into it.

She rushed from the room and checked the basement.

When she peaked down the old, rickety steps, she saw the lower half of her mother. The pain swelled in her head. "Ah!" she seethed through her teeth.

"June?"

"It's me," was all she could manage. Her mother climbed the steps in powerful strides.

"June, what's the matter? What are you doing here?"

She guided June back into the kitchen. June didn't open her eyes. She couldn't, the pain was too much. Each time she tried, a hundred punches rocked her skull.

"Call grandma," she managed.

Her mother grabbed her by the shoulders, gently. "Oh, honey, what's the matter? Another headache?"

June shot her head up, summoning a stunning pain that could split her in two. "Call her, please," she sobbed. "Please."

Snot ran from her nose. Her whole face throbbed.

"Please, please," she wept.

Her mother moved for the phone, though she didn't take her eyes off June. "What happened?"

June shook her head. The emerging truth was too terrible to deliver.

"Hello, operator?" her mother said. "Operator?"

But they were too late. June knew it. They'd been too late from the get-go. Because this vision, this nightmare, had already happened.

That was what she hated most about *the sense.*

It never came in time to help anyone. She could only watch in helpless horror.

She sobbed.

The man's gloved hands came into view, far away and from another time, like a horror show, and she saw them, once again, as they shoved her frail grandmother. She watched her grandmother fall back with an unnerving crack and squelch.

Blood shined on the corner of her grandmother's nightstand. Her pill organizer crashed to the floor, the little white tablets sticking to the growing pool of blood beneath her grandmother's head. Her eyes stared to the ceiling, unfeeling, dead.

Her mother must've received the news because her face had gone pale. Her usual assuredness melted into a frown. Right as her mouth opened, a piercing shriek sliced through the air.

June sat there as the tea kettle on the stove and her mother, telephone in hand, screamed.

CHAPTER THREE

Wednesday, August 5, 1959

10:30 AM

In the very church that condemned June's grandmother for her absence, June stood between the open doors. Down the aisle, in front of all the pews, and up a few steps, sat her grandmother's casket. The white satin-lined lid yawned open, revealing the pallid woman prepared with cotton balls in her cheeks for fullness, her mouth glued or sutured, June didn't know which, and makeup applied with a heavy hand. Her arms lay crossed at her stomach, holding white lilies.

June hated that this was normal. She didn't want to go look upon her dead grandmother. She'd already done that. Again and again, since her murder. Reliving the intruder's entry, the rummaging and ransacking, her grandmother's shuffling slippers, the fatal shove, the crack of a fractured skull. The blood. The tea kettle and her mother's scream.

But more than anything, June was angry. The police had no suspects, though they said similar burglaries had been happening in that area over the past several months. This report didn't console June or her mother. It infuriated both of them. If her grandmother had known someone was breaking into homes nearby, she might've locked the front door.

The police had tried to justify the lack of communication between the community and the officers responding to and investigating the break-ins. There hadn't been a lot of urgency. The intruder hadn't hurt anyone else. Hadn't even been seen.

"So why did she die, then?" June's mother had shouted.

When the wide-eyed officers, anxious and fidgeting, didn't answer, June did.

"Because she was home. And she fought back."

Then it was back to the detail her mother fixated upon.

"Why didn't she ever lock that goddamn door?" June had overhead her mother weep to her father as they dressed for the funeral, as well as the night before.

"Come on, Elaine. Try to get some sleep."

But her mother didn't. Couldn't. June had heard her pacing in the next room over. Coming up and down the stairs. Her mother would lock the doors and windows, only to wake up in fear that she'd forgotten and had to get up and check.

But to be fair to her grandmother, they hardly locked their front door either. Most didn't. It was a small town and everyone knew everyone. Burglaries like this were reserved for noir thrillers in theatres or frightful stories about the *big city*, Indianapolis or Chicago.

But now law enforcement had begun encouraging townspeople to lock their doors over the radios and in passing as they patrolled the town.

June gritted her teeth whenever she heard the warning that came too late for her grandmother.

She and her family stood before her grandmother's casket following the service. School teachers, old babysitters, family friends and long-distance family offered consoling nods and reassurances.

"So sorry for your loss," one of her father's co-workers said, shaking his hand like they might at the conclusion of a business meeting.

"Any update from the police?" a particularly insufferable long-distance and long-forgotten cousin asked June's mother.

June sighed, dread sitting in her throat like she'd dry-swallowed a thick pill.

"She's in a better place," one man said, eyeing June's dead grandmother in the casket.

A woman June recognized as one of the most devout church members in town took June's hands and said, " Your grandmother Rita was so lovely, though we missed her at Sunday service."

She too was insufferable.

June thought she might explode when a hand grabbed the back of her arm.

She snapped, trying to twist herself out of the grasp.

"Hey."

June was overwhelmed with relief. She threw herself into her friend's arms. "Vincent," she said.

He didn't apologize for her grandmother's death or pry into the details of the investigation. He just shared the silence with June. Her mind had been racing ever since she bolted from the school track, trying to hurry home and outrun death.

Additional arms wrapped around the pair of them. Lenny, Stef, Arthur, and Ingrid. June wanted to stay in that embrace forever.

The group parted. Lenny pulled at the neck of a collared shirt, beneath a black blazer. Stef wore a black skirt with dark stockings. Ingrid adorned something similar. They were all dressed for the occasion. All looking polished and proper. Arthur had tried to tame his blonde curls to no avail. Vincent even wore a tie.

June preferred Vincent in his usual leather jacket and auto-grease-stained jeans. And Lenny in his red and black letterman sweater. Stef in pastels. And Ingrid with a cigarette between her lips. She still wore her bright red lipstick, and it was the tiniest hint of normalcy June needed in that very unreal situation.

"Thanks for coming," June said. Angst melted from her and she relaxed her shoulders, stood a little taller.

"We all loved Rita," Stef said.

"And her cooking," Lenny said, which got a laugh from the group.

"I wish we were in her kitchen right now, waiting on cookies," Vincent said.

"Or her mashed potatoes," Arthur added.

"I'd take her feeding me spoonfuls of sour kraut. Anything beats this," June said, looking at her grandmother's casket.

She tried to imagine her grandmother with her hand-knitted pot holders, pulling a tray of her famous chocolate chip cookies from the oven.

Instead, she saw her on the ground, blood sputtering from her mouth, spilling from her head, seeping into the floorboards.

"June," her mother called. "Come say your last goodbyes."

Her mother looked to the casket. June stepped forward, looking down on her grandmother. She had the urge to hold her hand one final time. But she knew no warmth remained.

She knew what she'd feel if she touched the dead. She'd felt it once before as a child, when her grandfather, Rita's husband, had died. At the funeral, June had taken his dead hand. She'd hoped she'd see memories between the two of them. Summer afternoons on the front porch, waiting for the cheery tune of the ice cream truck. But instead, she'd felt ice shoot into her heart. She'd clutched her chest, drawing critical eyes from the mourners. She'd gasped. The emptiness of her grandfather's touch, the silence of his mind, the finality of his closed eyes, had crept within her and left her hollow for days. She couldn't eat. She couldn't sleep. She'd locked herself in her room and feared she'd never come out again.

That was the day she'd lost faith in God, the Devil, Heaven and Hell.

Nothing came after death.

Nothing at all.

That infinite void frightened her. She imagined herself floating in endless black, further and further from the life she'd known.

Since then, her sense had grown even stronger. She couldn't risk it. She retracted her hand and nodded to her parents.

Taking notice of her distress, June's friends ushered her to a bench in the lobby.

There they sat and shared the silence as mourners shuffled in and out.

Finally, Stef spoke.

"Are you still coming Friday?"

"Stef," Vincent said. "Come on. That's the last thing on her mind."

Stef looked to June. "I'm sorry. I only meant . . . I know horror films are your favorite."

June nodded and mustered a slight smile. "We'll see."

Ingrid adjusted in her seat, considering this. "You know, June, it might actually be good for you."

And thinking about it, the monsters onscreen and hopefully Vincent Price, granted her a moment's relief.

Ingrid was right. June would need the distraction, the comfort of her friends. She needed to go.

Friday, August 7, 1959
6:23 PM

"We're really glad you came, June," Ingrid said, offering her a consoling smile as June climbed into the Studebaker.

"Yeah," Stef echoed. "The DUSK TIL DAWN SPOOK-TACULAR was made for you."

June gasped upon seeing her reflection in the rearview mirror of Ingrid's Studebaker. It was ghostly, her skin waxen, dead and doll-like.

June smoothed her ponytail, feeling a little grime of the previous day's hairspray. She'd touched up her bangs, but she couldn't stand to look at herself in the mirror too much longer. Each time she did, she saw her grandmother just behind her. Blood oozing down the side of her face like thick sap.

She gave up trying to fix herself and sank back in the seat.

"Let me help," Stef offered. "Turn around so I can fix your ponytail."

June turned on the red bench, her back to Stef.

June's and Ingrid's eyes met. The pity had dimmed the usual brightness in Ingrid's.

Don't look at me like that, June wanted to say.

Something rolled under the vehicle, pulling Ingrid's attention back to the road.

She overcorrected and passed into the opposite lane. Stef caught herself against the passenger door and June nearly crashed into her.

"What the hell was that?" Ingrid said once she straightened the vehicle.

Then, they saw the road ahead sprinkled with fallen limbs. Ingrid zigzagged around them.

"You'd think they'd have cleared these by now," Stef said.

Stef retrieved a hairbrush from her bag and released the black ribbon in June's hair, letting it fall past her shoulders.

Ingrid clicked on the radio and was met with static. She scanned and found Doris Day's "Stay On The Right Side, Sister." She turned the volume knob up.

June's heart beat to the rhythm of the snappy swing song.

The car cruised down a lone road. It was clearer than some of the back roads before and curtained by gargantuan, green corn stalks. On the other side were trees, some toppled in on one another, limbs scattered and stacked like bodies in a mass grave.

The Studebaker came upon a long line of cars stalled ahead of them and rolled to a stop. Doo-wop tunes played over radios and out open windows. Teens leaned out of cars, waving and shouting to friends in nearby vehicles, only to quickly duck back in to avoid getting sprayed with mud.

Stef sank the teeth of the brush into June's hair. Her shoulders relaxed as her friend worked through each knot with patience. When she ran the brush from June's scalp to the ends, she felt more at peace than she had in days.

Stef brushed June's hair into her hand and tied it up. Then, she swiped a mauve dime store blush over June's cheeks and did a light powder dusting over the "shiny" parts of her face.

When June checked her reflection once more, she found that she recognized a different part of herself. One that wasn't so afraid and grief-stricken, so exhausted from nightmares and never-ending pangs of guilt.

"Hmm," Stef said. "Now, how about some lipstick?"

Mud flung against the side of Ingrid's car. She pressed the gas and they momentarily sunk.

"Come on," Ingrid said.

She turned the wheel and the car rolled up out of the rut.

"I can't imagine how flooded the lot will be," Ingrid said.

The tires trudged through the thick, goopy mud. Ingrid was easy on the gas. Stef would've gunned it right away. June didn't know how to drive and she didn't want to learn. What if a vision struck her, pulling her away from the wheel, the car free to cross lanes into oncoming traffic? The other driver sent soaring through the windshield?

Other times she dreamed of a child chasing a ball and, in a second, the boy's head a mushy mess of meat against the asphalt, his mother screaming from the front porch. All because someone else's pain, some other disturbance, had pulled her away.

A car behind them stalled and then roared back to life. The passengers cheered and the emerging line of moviegoers rolled by a scattering of sticks piled high at the edges of the drowning drive, and past the unlit Peterson's Pictures lettering and marquee beneath. In bold block letters, it read *DUSK TIL DAWN SPOOKTACULAR!*

Finally, they reached the little ticket shack. This light, too, had not yet flicked on. There was still an hour until sunset. Ingrid tried to roll down her window, but the crank stuck. She gripped it with both hands and tugged, the window finally giving way and rolling down as she spun the handle.

She flashed a sheepish smile at the ticket window attendant. "Stupid window's always sticking. Three adults, please."

"Hey, look who it is," Stef said.

It was William, the shy boy from their school, son of the pastor, who apparently went skinny dipping with Annie. June couldn't imagine what the two of them could possibly have in common. Or that he'd be bold enough to sneak out and go skinny dipping in the middle of the night.

"Gone swimming lately, William?" Ingrid teased.

June nudged her. "Leave him alone."

William stared at them. He was horrified.

With blazing red cheeks, he counted heads and said, "That'll be three dollars, please."

Stef leaned across June. "Three dollars!"

"Jeepers," June said. But it could've cost her all of her savings; she wouldn't have missed this. Even with what happened on Monday. Especially because of what happened. She needed this.

Like Stef said, horror films were her favorite.

"Sorry, erm . . ." William fumbled the parking ticket roll and hardly had enough space to bend over and retrieve them. He had crazy long legs that some of the guys hoped would turn him into a strong basketball player—basketball was *the* sport in Indiana—but he was the most uncoordinated gangly thing she'd ever seen.

Ingrid collected the cash from her friends and handed it to William. His blonde flattop was greasy with too much product.

June thought if he let up on the grease, went with a more relaxed 'do, *nice* girls might talk to him. Girls who wouldn't only be with him in the dark.

William tore a parking stub and passed it to Ingrid. "It's a little extra for the all-night show."

"Oh, that's alright," Ingrid said, batting those wild, long lashes. She eased off the break. "William, you've been an absolute doll." She pursed her red lips, making a *smooch* sound.

He blushed. "Enjoy the—oh, wait a sec!" he said. He grabbed a bunch of green plastic bags.

Ingrid stared at him, amused.

"Vomit bags," William said, delighting in their attention. "You know, because the films might be *just too terrifying to stomach!*" He was having fun with it, and June shared his excitement.

"You're so full of baloney," Stef said, though June and Ingrid knew she was already spooked.

They pulled away from the ticket booth and drove the path to the lot. Vehicles already lined the front row and half the second. The bottom trim of each was splattered with mud. June knew a few greasers were fuming over the state of their hot rods. She saw a few outside their vehicles, wiping at small spots with dust rags. Another licked his thumb and worked at a stubborn smudge of dirt on his driver side mirror.

At concessions stood three women in white knee-length dresses. Their hair was pulled back in tight buns, and topped with starch nurses' caps. Their brilliant, unstained shoes were a beacon, a *hey look at me,* amidst the mud-caked trail into the lot. The concession stand awning shielded them from the weather.

"Nurses? For what?" Stef said, the uneasiness elevating her voice to a higher, more childlike pitch.

"It's theater," Ingrid winked.

Stef frowned, her brows knitted.

They drove to a sloped spot near concessions on the outer rim of the lot and unbuckled. The parking space to their right was the first in the segregated section for Black patrons. Mr. Peterson hadn't enforced this rule, but a local policeman named Officer Reed did. Another vehicle sat in this section. A Black man sat behind the wheel.

June recognized the cool purple color of his car. She'd seen it parked at the bakery near Lenny's house. This man was the owner. He made the best beignets June had ever had. Lenny's mother ordered huge batches of them for Easter Sunday dinner, Lenny's sister's bridal shower, Fourth of July barbecues, you name it. Beignets were one of the best things about attending Lenny's parents' gatherings. June's parents thought so, too.

Lenny's mother had brought a package of beignets for June and her family the evening after the funeral. She was such a good woman. Lenny was like her in so many ways.

"Whoa!" Ingrid exclaimed.

The excitement tugged June from the memory.

Just beneath the screen sat the black, low-slung body of a hearse. A clever, theatrical reminder of mortality, June thought. Not that she needed it.

Behind the screen was an entanglement of fallen limbs. Miraculously, none had caused any damage. Though they created a hell of a backdrop for a horror show.

"Okay, the hearse gives me the creeps," Stef said.

"They're just being prepared," June said.

Stef was quiet. And then Ingrid broke out laughing and June couldn't help herself.

"Very funny, you guys," Stef sneered, crossing her arms.

Ingrid killed the engine. "Where are the boys?"

The mention of *boys* revived Stef. Chipper once more. "They'll be here." She fished for a compact in her bag, dabbing here and there.

"Yeah, yeah. You're gorgeous," Ingrid said. "Get the speaker."

Stef cranked her window down to retrieve the metal-cased speaker attached to a post. Each parking spot had two, serving two adjacent cars. Vincent, Lenny, and Arthur would take its twin when they showed. Stef stretched the retractable cord and clipped it to the window and turned the dial.

"Is it man . . . or monster?" a booming showman said over the speaker. "The answer may be too terrifying to know!"

A villainous voice, groaning and cackling, came over the speakers.

Ingrid poked at Stef. They swatted at one another, giggling.

Organ music played throughout the lot, which brought forth images of haunted mansions and Gothic castles.

"And now for tonight's lineup," the showman said.

"Shhh," June said, "I want to hear what pictures they're showing."

The recording continued, "Tonight's features include William Castle's *buzzing* film, *The Tingler*, starring Vincent Price. *Cat People* starring Simone Simon. And then back to the master of menace.

"That's right, we've got more scares from Mr. Price, ladies and gents. You'll see him as a *murderous* psychiatrist, alongside Lynn Bari, in *Shock*. As an eccentric billionaire hosting a haunted house party in another William Castle picture, *House On Haunted Hill*, and finally as the vengeful, body-snatching wax sculptor in *House of Wax*."

June stomped her feet against the floorboard in a little happy dance. Vincent Price and William Castle were her favorites. She couldn't have picked better films herself.

"And then we have *Curse of the Demon* and lastly, a teen-scream favorite, *The Blob! Beware of the Blob!*"

An echo of screams exploded from the speaker.

"*TERROR*," he said, maniacally. *"And other tricks and treats! So, scream! Scream!"*

Arriving movie goers did just that. The horror fans could've shaken the town with their hoots and hollers and wolfish howls. Stef shrank closer to June and away from the speaker.

"Hours of this?"

"Dusk til Dawn, sweetie," Ingrid said with an unlit cigarette wagging between her lips.

This was reviving June's spirit. She nudged Stef with a smile. "It's all night fright!"

Something pushed the car forward. Stef gasped. "What was that?"

Just then, something pounced against Stef's door. A big hand shot past the speaker and reached for her. Stef pressed her back into June, her feet on the seat, kicking away from the door. She closed her eyes and squealed.

Her door opened and she kicked harder.

"Whoa, Stef," Lenny said, raising his hands up in defense. "It's me."

Lenny wore his black and red letterman sweater, despite the heat, and he had the biggest, melting brown eyes that Stef told June and Ingrid she'd fallen in love with at first glance. To June, it gave Lenny this sort of teddy bear quality. Reflective of his kind heart.

Stef stopped kicking and sat up. Her terror morphed into confusion before solidifying into anger.

"What're you doing scaring me like that? Huh?"

She swatted at him.

June and Ingrid laughed.

Lenny eventually coaxed Stef into the backseat of the Studebaker with him. He leaned against the window. Stef rested against his broad chest, though she wasn't quite ready to forgive him for frightening her.

"It's not funny," Stef said, but she couldn't help but smile when Lenny wrapped his arms around her.

"Lenny, you got a lighter?" Ingrid asked from the front seat. He reached intoe his pocket, crinkling the green plastic vomit bag he'd received at the ticket window, too. It fell to the floorboard.

"Sorry, Ingrid." Lenny shrugged, pockets emptied. "Ask Vincent."

Stef crossed her arms. "You hopped out early, just to scare me?"

The rest of the guys would get an earful about conspiring. But June loved it, scaring as a team effort. That's why she hoped to work on horror pictures some day. She wanted to give people more than entertainment. That's what William Castle and Vincent Price were all about. Horror as an experience—*Percepto!*

Additional vehicles pulled into the lot. And just a couple rows ahead, parked diagonally from them, was a red Chevy Bel Air. It belonged to the town doctor. Annie's father.

"Hey, check it out," Stef said. She sat up and pointed to the Chevy. "It's Annie."

"That girl's meaner than a snake," Lenny said. Even he'd had bouts of bullshit with Annie. Most of the gang had. Most of the school had. Staff, too.

"A bucket of popcorn says she's waiting for William," Ingrid said.

"The ticket booth kid?" Lenny asked, bewildered.

"Oh yeah." Stef grinned. "They're *friendlier* than you know."

Before any of the girls could elaborate further, Vincent pulled up in the sloped spot to their right. The first in the segregated section. He waved to the baker whom he'd nicknamed Dr. Sweets. The old man loved it.

Arthur sat in the backseat, blowing smoke rings from a cigar he'd stolen from his father. Where Vincent was the tough greaser type, with gelled black hair and rugged and stained jeans, Arthur was more laid back. Unkempt in a boyish way.

Vincent got out of the truck and pulled the retractable speaker from its post and attached it to his window.

"They started all the fun without us." He hopped a puddle and headed for June's side of the Studebaker. "Did they already say what flicks they're showin'?"

He smoothed his hair and retrieved the cigarette from behind his ear.

"Some of the best," June said. "They're playing *The Tingler*! And *Shock*!"

Arthur came around the truck and to the Studebaker. "I heard *House On Haunted Hill,* too. How come they're not showing any monster flicks?"

He meant the Universal monster movies. Arthur loved *Werewolf of London.*

"There's all kinds of monsters," Vincent said.

June nodded with approval. "You'll love *Shock*," she promised.

She and Vincent had seen *Shock* at the drive-in when they were only kids. Their mothers assumed they were fast asleep in their sleeping bags in the backseat, but they'd sat up for most of the show. As their mothers passed a bottle of wine back and forth, taking long sips, they watched Vincent Price's face harden with anger as he swung a candlestick at his wife, declaring his hatred of her.

"It's good to see you here," Vincent said, giving a knowing smile.

Ingrid sighed, exasperated. "Does anyone have a lighter?"

Arthur tossed a matchbook into the car.

The sour impatience on Ingrid's face dissolved as she held the flame to the cigarette and inhaled smoke. She passed the cigarette to June, who was especially careful of the glowing embers at its end. She noticed the tip was stained apple red with a perfect impression of the curves of Ingrid's lips. She brought her own around the cigarette.

"Guys, look." Lenny sat up, hands over the front seat, to get a better look. A fog unfurled just beneath the screen, which flashed electric bolts and a reminder to return your speaker to the post before pulling away. The front rows of headlights produced a yellow haze effect. It flowed down and hugged the hearse, crawling around its tires.

"Spooky," June mused.

"Did you see that? There's someone in the fog back there," Arthur said, pointing.

A man in black stepped too far into the light, revealing coolers at his sides. When he placed them beside the hearse and opened the lid, he hurried away from it.

"Dry ice," Ingrid observed.

"I love it," June said.

Vincent drummed against Ingrid's car. "We better split if we're going to hit concessions before the show."

June collected orders and coins from everyone and snatched her purse from the floorboard. Just as she slammed the car door, a black Ford Interceptor pulled up behind the two vehicles. Blocking them in.

Officer Reed planted a black cowboy boot into the mud. Despite being only a deputy, Officer Reed carried the big-headed prowess of a Western flick's town sheriff.

He approached them, his wooden baton waving at his side.

"Come to see the spook show?" Vincent asked, crossing his arms. He was the muscle, the smooth-talker, and she was the insurance, the good kid whose presence set *most* adults at ease. But Officer Reed was different. When Vincent was caught speeding down the wrong side of the road racing against Arthur, Officer Chapin pulled the boys aside, straightened them out, and sent them on their way. Same when he'd caught Ingrid with brandy in her soda. He never came looking to see if kids were causing trouble. If he found them in it, he talked to them, made sure they got home safe, and went on with his day. Officer Reed, on the other hand, brewed trouble where there was none. Craved it, even.

"Starting trouble already?" he scolded.

"We're parked on the edges, bumping shoulders with the trees damn near," Vincent interjected. They weren't parked quite as far over as they typically did, with the excessive flooding and debris.

Officer Reed approached Vincent, carelessly swinging his hickory baton. He stopped far too close to June and Vincent.

"You are right on the line. Which means *he* is absolutely out of bounds in *that* vehicle." He pointed to Ingrid's car with a sneer.

Officer Reed kicked his cowboy boots in the mud. "If he's not in that truck when I come back 'round, your friend's bought himself a ticket to the clink. Understand?"

"We'll take care of it," June said. She turned to Ingrid's car and saw Stef peeking out the rear window. Her face was flushed. Lenny had been carted off by Officer Reed on several occasions and sat behind bars until Officer Chapin discovered him and drove him home.

Lenny emerged from the Studebaker and walked right beside Officer Reed's vehicle, avoiding the brute's glowering stare, and climbed into Vincent's truck.

Officer Reed raised his eyebrows. "Smart kid." He lingered for a moment, long enough to let the threatening swell of his presence, and the promise of his return, settle deep into their bones.

Officer Reed slunk back into his car and drove off, flinging mud behind him. June and Vincent raised their arms to shield themselves.

Friday, August 7, 1959
7:12 PM

C oncessions were in a small white building near the rear of the lot. It was another reason the gang always parked where they had.

"What's a movie without popcorn?" June said, trying to calm things. She brushed away caked mud from her face and arms. Vincent had some on his face, just below his dark and deep widow's peak. He abrasively swiped it away.

"Guy's such a schmuck."

June agreed.

Yellow string lights squared off each of the six windows of the concession stand. Five nurses stood between each. None of whom June recognized, though she knew several in town. Her grandmother had one visit every week before she passed.

These nurses were actresses.

"Make sure to grab some snacks so you don't get woozy," one of the nurses advised customers waiting in line. Another passed out additional green vomit bags. Eager men drawn to the bubbly blondes took several bags, Vincent included.

"You're a ham," June teased.

When a short nurse with dark hair and fair skin caught her attention, June blushed.

Vincent saw.

"Oh, you're one to talk."

The beautiful nurse reminded June of a glass china doll she'd had atop a bedroom shelf. Her grandmother gifted it to her on her twelfth birthday. June never had the heart to tell her that it frightened her.

The doll and nurse shared fair skin, with rose-red painted lips, and a disturbing and robotic exuberance highlighted by a peachy-pink shimmer on the cheek bones.

June turned away and, on the screen behind her, she watched popcorn with bright eyes, arms, and legs dance. A hot dog waltzed behind it, then a pretzel with bold feminine eyelashes. Block letters fell above them:

LET'S GET A TREAT! VISIT OUR CONCESSIONS!

As the sun slowly sank into the horizon, the lot became a sea of headlights and theatrical string lights. *The Blob* theme song played overhead. June tapped her foot to the beat.

"Next!" an acne-plagued teen called.

She and Vincent shuffled forward. The couple ahead of them, a few years older than they were, chatted about Elvis Presley serving overseas. Most couldn't imagine a celebrity like him in uniform. But it happened. June was sure Presley wasn't the only one.

The screen blinked to life. A cartoon, against a mustard-yellow backdrop, showed a family; a blonde woman, a small child with an ice cream cone, and a man carrying an infant. They ran from the concessions to a cartoon projector. It looped as a timer sank to the top center of the screen. An accompanying message read, Show starts in ten minutes.

"We only have ten minutes," June said, antsy. She swatted at a mosquito zipping in front of her face.

The line continued to move until it was finally Vincent and June's turn. June turned over her shoulder and caught the peculiar nurse still transfixed on her. Any attraction she'd felt before was devoured by trepidation. Her skin prickled, but she couldn't look away.

"Good grief." Vincent put his arm around June and swept her aside as an older brother would. Only then did the nurse shift her gaze to the patrons ahead, still unblinking.

Behind the counter, a team of teens they recognized from town and school hustled around the deep fryers, shaking fries and dumping fresh potatoes into the bubbling oil. Others hollered orders, sending a petite girl with braids to fetch steaming, hot burgers from the grill. She hurried to the grill and reached for the spatula. Grease-slickened, it slid through her hand. When she tried to catch it, she hit her fist against the edge of the grill. She yelped.

Heat blistered on June's hand. "Ah," she gasped.

The girl hurried to the kitchen sink, bumping a tub of popcorn to the floor.

June's skin tightened, radiating intense heat. She inspected the area with her fingers. No burn. Just the usual phantom pain, like when Janice broke her ankle.

An older woman with round dollops of blush on her cheeks fussed with the faucet for the girl.

Their concession attendant at their window asked, "She alright?"

The woman, noticing the patrons looking on, smiled and gave a thumbs up.

The attendant redirected his attention to Vincent.

"Sorry 'bout that. What can I get for you?"

"Three family-sized popcorns, four root beers, one cotton candy, and—" he leaned away from the window, "June, what did Lenny want?"

"Just popcorn," she said, eyes still on the poor girl. Their attendant filled their popcorn himself and moments later their arms were full of refreshments. "I hope that girl wasn't burned too badly."

They trudged through the mud, the soles of their shoes thick with it, and Vincent was beaming.

"What?"

He tossed a glance over his shoulder at the china doll nurse. "I think someone is sweet on you."

June met her eyes one last time and felt her breath catch in her throat. She swallowed the knot and flitted past Vincent. She dispelled her discomfort with squeals of excitement as she reached the cars. They found Ingrid alone in her vehicle. Lenny and Stef were in the front seat of Vincent's truck, with Arthur reclined in the backseat, hands behind his head, surrounded by clouds from his cigar.

Just as they settled in, the screen cut to black. Then, a man, short and stout, emerged, and crackling film lines pulsed around him. He faced the audience directly.

"Ladies and gentleman, poor souls who have braved the terror ahead, I must warn you, the film you are about to see . . ." He paused as if at a loss for words. ". . . is one of betrayal, lies, and, most regrettably, murder."

He shook his bald head, dismayed. "Some of you may become nauseated by what you're about to see onscreen. Upon arrival, you received one of these." The producer waved a vomit bag in front of the camera, his face obscured. The crinkling was so juvenile, but unsettling.

Patrons in rag tops cheered and threw their vomit bags to the sky. As if present, the producer closed his hand around the bag, holding everyone in silence. "Now, hang onto these in the event that you become so disturbed, so unraveled by the film you are about to see, that you need to expel all that displeasure."

Audience members sized one another up, identifying those most susceptible to such an ailment. June shoved handfuls of popcorn into her mouth. The man absorbed her attention. She wasn't thinking about her grandmother or the strange nurse. Horror films had that effect on her. It was like listening to a song that just fills you up, makes you warm. It was energizing. Magnetic, even.

The man in the suit and tie continued, "I hope you all have your affairs in order." He signed his initials on a document titled **Will & Testament,** which made the audience *ooo.* "Because tonight may be your very last." He capped his pen. The dramatic sweeping of an organ ensued.

"How cheerful," Ingrid chimed. She reached for June's popcorn, her second cigarette of the night in her other hand.

"Nurses are stationed nearby to help," the man said. "But I fear, for some of you, it's already too late." He looked down, drawing everyone's eyes to the hearse parked just below the screen.

"I bet Stef is about ready to call it," Vincent said. They turned their heads and, sure enough, saw Stef cuddled up to Lenny, a green vomit bag clutched in her hands.

The projector came to life with the screaming floating head of a teen. Vincent startled, sending popcorn flying from the backseat and into the windshield. Another screaming head joined, a girl this time, her shrieks dire and alarming.

"Scream! Scream!" the producer repeated in a foreboding tone.

A man in front of them ejected himself from the driver's side of his car and spewed chunks into the mud, neglecting his vomit bag. He fell onto his hands and knees. The blonde nurse June had seen before rushed from concessions. Before she even checked the "patient," she put her hands up and shouted, "Settle down, everyone. There's no need for alarm."

The china doll nurse scurried over and knelt at the man's side. "Help me get him up," the blonde woman said. An overhead light flicked off, shrouding the scene in darkness, and the audience shrieked and gasped.

With the flick of a switch, the light illuminated the same vehicle, where the man had been sick, but when the nurses came to their feet, it wasn't the man standing between them.

It was a skeleton.

The audience exploded into cheers and screams.

CHAPTER SIX

This was June's second time seeing *The Tingler*, but it captivated her just the same. William Castle was absolutely brilliant. A master of horror as *entertainment*. She wished she could've seen the picture in the theatre so she could have experienced the *Percepto!* trick people were buzzing about.

Audience members *ooo*-ed and *ahh*-ed as a deaf and mute theater-owner named Martha, played by Judith Evelyn, returned home to a series of frights, including a hatchet-hurling monster and a hand reaching at her from the bathtub full of blood. A foil for the woman's blood phobia and inability to scream due to a lack of vocal chords.

June leaned back, eating popcorn by the fistful, as the pathologist, Vincent Price, began his autopsy. She loved this part.

The creature exposed!

But something nagged at her and carried her away from Price wrestling with the Tingler. She'd always sensed people's discomfort in a way, but this sensation was new to her. It didn't feel quite like pain, not like she had in that fleeting moment at the concession stand when her hand blistered. Nor was it like what she had felt when her grandmother was killed.

This was something else. A straining of sorts.

"You guys okay?" she asked.

"Just hungry," Vincent complained from the backseat. "*Someone* already ate through the popcorn."

She ignored Vincent's bellyaching and turned to Ingrid. "And you?"

"Fine," she assured June.

June looked to Vincent's truck beside them, full of her friends.

"They're fine too, ya know?" Ingrid said.

June smiled. Her friend knew her all too well. June settled back into her seat.

Price had done it. Peeled the insectoid away from Martha's spine. Its silhouette from behind the examination screen squirmed.

"Ick!" Stef shouted from the truck.

In the distance, just beneath one of the tall lights near the screen, a beastly man fell from the driver's seat of a vehicle shaped like a Buick Roadmaster—too far to know for certain. He made no effort to catch himself, his extremities limp, as if he'd fainted. Perfect timing for the gag since the pathologist onscreen had just removed the Tingler from the woman's spine.

June expected him to come to, position himself on his hands and knees and vomit like the actor before had. Instead, he lay flat on the grass, legs sprawled. The blonde nurse dutifully headed where she was needed.

"Please, don't be alarmed," she repeated as she made her way around the vehicles. She passed Ingrid's open window. "Please don't be alarmed. Remain seated."

The crowd mumbled.

"No, I think he's really fainted," June heard a man say.

"You suppose those are *real* nurses?" another inquired with a trembling voice.

Vincent sprang up from the back seat and pointed. "June, look. It's your girl."

Where there might have been butterflies in her stomach before, June felt her insides roil, thickening like sap. She put a hand over her gut, a self-soothing technique she knew didn't help.

Moments later, the china doll nurse emerged from behind the vehicle. Her gaze remained stoic, and June wondered if that's what the actress thought it took to play a nurse that's seen it all. But the woman went out of her way, with the man and fellow nurse straight ahead, to pass June. She looked into the vehicle, as one might, casually, but those eyes . . . When they met June's, she felt pressure double down on her spine.

Screams exploded from the screen as the Tingler was free of its cage.

When the china doll nurse reached the man on the ground, she knelt at his side. She pounded her hands against his sternum. Chest compressions did not, however, appear to revive the man.

"My god, he's dead!" a man shouted. June wasn't sure whether he was an actor or spectator. Same of the man on the ground.

The light above popped off. The nurses and patrons were not quite concealed in the dark. They had another fifteen minutes or so before the sun would set completely. Yet, this tactic was still effective. It offered the threat of stolen visibility come nightfall.

Actors on screen urged the audience to scream for their lives!

Shrieks exploded from the speakers across the lot and the patrons joined in, creating a cacophony of both terror and delight.

Even Ingrid joined in, bellowing a howl. Lenny hung from the driver side of Vincent's truck and cheered, pounding his fist against the dash. This, of course, unnerved Vincent.

"Easy!" Vincent cried from the backseat to Lenny.

Stef shrieked, though the fear in her voice added a shaky, unconvincing vibrato. Arthur roared over her. Then it became a screaming match between the Studebaker and the truck.

June had practiced her horror scream in the basement several times when her parents were out. She employed it then, feeling like she was in the pictures herself. It was exhilarating, she thought, scaring others to death.

The exuberance was short lived as brief sounds isolated from the rest of the noise and found June.

Gasping. Gurgling. Choking.

June coughed as if vestiges of the fog had crept into her lungs. The air thick and swollen, determined not to escape her mouth. Her friends didn't take notice. They obeyed the repeated commands booming from the car speakers, "Scream! Scream!"

Gasping. Choking.

June wheezed and hacked into her fist. Blood pounded in her ears like the orchestral drums of a Rita Hayworth song. A kicking rhythm made to make people move.

She knew how Judith Evelyn's character felt. Every nerve in her body ignited with sharp pricks. Everything in her said, *Scream*. But her breath was slow to return. She mustered a short-lived whimper. Her head felt light on her neck, like it might just roll off and onto the floorboard.

June covered her ears.

Moments later, the lights jolted awake like lightning, and Ingrid must've seen the distress on June's face as she uncovered her ears.

"Well don't scream yourself silly," Ingrid said.

When June looked up, she saw that the blonde nurse was gone. Only the china doll nurse remained, her petite shadow elongated over the man at her feet, devouring him in a blanket of darkness. The peculiar actress made for his feet. She took one foot in each of her dainty, pale hands, and pulled. The man's arms were forced over his head from the momentum but were lifeless just the same. No one moved to assist her. Through the thick mud, the petite china doll nurse dragged the man between the cars. Mud seeped into the Buick driver's white t-shirt, stained with condiments and burger drippings. The crowd was astonished. And amused.

"Shit," Vincent said. "That guy has to be heavy." He leaned forward. "June, how ya think they're doing that?"

June had no idea. "I've never seen anything like it."

Audience members rose from their seats and hung out their windows to see. Teens stood in their rag tops, clinking bottles without paying any mind to the wandering police officer. Viewers pointed and laughed as the nurse with the dead eyes that always found June adjusted her grip, sinking the man's head further into the muck, and lugged him away. There was no effort to protect or preserve him as the china doll nurse heaved him over debris and through murky puddles. Water splashed against the nurse's shins, but she didn't care or didn't notice.

The ruckus followed the pair all the way to the rear of the lot, just between Ingrid and Vincent's vehicles, where the nurse stopped, brushing her hands over her clinically clean uniform, leaving a rust-colored residue. Much darker than the stuff William Castle used in the bathtub scene. Mud maybe?

June couldn't look away. No one could. Nor could they stop laughing. Everyone except June, whose effort to relax and enjoy the fun was quaking with angst. The nurse straightened her back and turned so her eyes met June's. This time, the nurse dipped her chin with a wicked grin, and what might've appeared to be an awkward attraction before now seemed sinister.

Then, she carried on, dragging the man away. Most of the audience returned their attention to the screen, including Ingrid and Arthur. But June squinted through the rear window, just off Vincent's shoulder, just long enough to see the nurse disappear into the darkness beyond the concession stand.

The end credits rolled and the screen cut to black. Then, the dancing snacks reappeared alongside the message in bold, bubbly letters: **Let's get a treat! Visit our concessions!**

Moviegoers hurried from their vehicles, dodging mud puddles, and formed a line at concessions. June followed them with her eyes. There was no sign of the china doll nurse.

"Well, I don't know about you two," Vincent said, "but all that screaming made me thirsty."

He pushed against June's seat, but she didn't budge. "Come on, June. Hurry up before the lines get too long."

Ingrid handed him a dollar bill. "More popcorn, too, please."

"Yeah, and this time, I get to be the popcorn keeper," Vincent teased, climbing from the Studebaker.

"June," Ingrid said, climbing from the vehicle, "let's hit the restrooms."

Lenny called from the truck, shaking kernels within his popcorn buckets. "Vince, think you can fill us up?"

Arthur came around the other side of the truck and grabbed the buckets. "I got it."

He looked at Vincent and June. "I'm sitting with you guys for the next show. The love birds are too much."

He pointed to the truck, and through the rear window, June saw Lenny and Stef's shadows meet.

Friday, August 7, 1959
7:13 PM

The creature clung to the bony ridges of its host's spine. A woman. It was getting better at distinguishing humans from one another. It was stronger now that it had been satiated, its thoughts clearer and more profound. But it needed more. And it wanted to be patient with this woman. This host felt more useful.

The creature had managed to access its host's operative system. It smiled, because the creature thought that's what upheld its humanness to the others. It pressed a pincer against the skin without piercing it, and the woman quaked with fear, but her will was too submerged to act upon it. How peculiar to see the host in such a way. How fascinating. It pressed the pincer a touch harder and the woman's limbs shot out before her. The creature leaned left and the host leaned left. It pressed forward and the host stepped forward.

It was surrounded by humans. But it wasn't afraid. Any fear it felt wasn't its own, it knew. It struck the creature then that it had chosen the right path. This was where it was meant to be.

It just had to keep going, keep feeding. It camouflaged easily to the woman's flesh and could slink down her spine if need be.

One human caught its eye, or maybe the eye of its host. The creature turned to see a young, blonde girl with a black ribbon in her hair. She smiled at the creature. It wanted to eat her already. But something was off about this being. Its warmth and entanglement of sounds and emotions stretched so far beyond what it recognized within humans.

The girl looked away. Was that fear on her face? Her warmth was clouded with it before the creature had even made a move.

The creature slept, returning the host's control of consciousness, though she'd have no recollection of the creature.

Not long into its rest, the creature was awoken by screams. Its host knelt beside a man.

The creature placed the woman's hands around the man's throat as the lights dimmed. With a vibrating, mounding strength, it shoved her thumbs into the man's throat, crushing what lay beneath with a *crack*. Guttural chokes soon turned to silence. The warmth went cold.

The creature released him, in disbelief of its own strength. Of how quickly life had vacated the man.

It remembered a purpose, a drive that it had misplaced before. It wasn't just here to kill, but to cause havoc. To create a show of its own. It had been given a chance at redemption. For what? It didn't know exactly, but it knew it would as it ate its way through the crowd.

Though, it wasn't done with this body yet. For it and its host had plenty left to do.

The creature steered the woman as she reached for the man's feet. Together, they pulled.

And as far as it could tell, the quick weight to the man's throat revealed no visible damage. The humans would be none the wiser. Good, it thought. For now, as it regained its strength, it needed anonymity.

When the creature reached the vehicle containing the strange girl with the blended and fractured energy, their eyes met. The creature forced a smile that its host resisted and failed.

It searched for dark and saw it beyond concessions, where it lugged away the dead human.

As it pulled the man into the shadows, a new warmth struck it.

A new human approached.

Tall, lanky, and thin.

The creature was grateful its appetite was for fear rather than flesh.

The laughter and wild screams on the other side of the trees died and gave way to a quirky, melodic tune.

The marquee blinked in and out, creating shadows before the ticket window, then blanketing them in darkness. On and Off. On and Off. It hummed with electrical strain.

William waited for *The Tingler* to end, and once he saw the familiar colors of the concession advertisement, he closed up shop. Peterson's Pictures had strict box office hours. No tickets sold after one hour into the show. However, this being the first DUSK TIL DAWN SPOOKTACULAR, they told him to allow in stragglers who came along during the first film.

William walked the lone path to the drive-in lot where Anna Lou waited for him in her red Chevrolet Bel Air. They agreed to catch *Cat People* once his shift ended.

William hadn't quite figured that girl out. She had an undeniable mean streak. He'd seen it. He'd seen her punch a girl square in the teeth the previous school year. He'd also seen her swap the failed test in her student mailbox with another student's. She'd erased and rewritten the names at the top. And when she got caught, boy did she raise hell.

She never seemed to unleash this rage upon William, though. Because of this, he began to think of *Annie* as someone else. *Annie* was a bully. *Annie* was so angry.

Anna Lou was different. Anna Lou teased him, but in a playful, intimate way, when they laid on their backs and floated in the ravine. Sometimes she'd sing for William. He loved to hear her sing Rita Hayworth and Doris Day songs.

Anna Lou, still tough as heck, would probably punch William if she heard him say it, but he thought he loved her.

Free-flowing vomit bags swirled around his feet in the wind. He still had several in his pocket. They sounded like whispers as they *swished, swished*. He thought of letting the rest go in the wind, but it felt wasteful. He didn't know what the Petersons paid for all the props and special effects. Maybe they'd want to use the leftovers for a double-feature horror night. He'd keep them, maybe make sure Anna Lou had one. She'd get a kick out of that.

Eventually, his lanky legs carried him around the trees and to the lot of cars. He headed for the concession stand at the back.

He noted the timer floating on the screen. He had ten minutes to get his stuff from the projector room storage closet, which doubled as the staff "locker room," and get to Anna Lou.

He noticed one of the actresses Mr. Peterson hired for the night, struggling with a prop of some kind. He drew nearer and saw the pale nurse dragging a large dummy around the concession windows.

"Need a hand?"

Wait. Is that—

As he came closer, William saw it was a man she pulled; not a dummy. He followed her past the bathroom, and to the back of the building.

"Wait," William said, hurrying after her.

He wanted to know if the man was okay. If the nurse was trying to get him away from the crowd for treatment.

She's an actress, William reminded himself.

He wanted to know how the actor remained so still. How the petite woman dragged him with impossible strength. The man's head clipped the edge of the building as she tugged him around.

The man looked so heavy.

There must've been some sort of rolling device beneath him, something the nurse slid in place. But if trucks and other automobiles struggled through the mud on the lot, William surmised whatever little wheels were on such a tool would too. When he caught up to the nurse, the door marked **STAFF ONLY** swung shut.

He reached for the handle with an uneasy hand. The motion, though he didn't know why, filled him with dread.

"Hello? Ma'am?"

There was no answer. And no one in sight. The usual yellow gloom from the dying overhead light fixture was off. Mr. Peterson usually left it on for him and the concession workers until they closed for the night. In fact, there was a note posted, reminding employees to leave the light on. The space doubled as a supply room for high intensity lamps used in the projector, fluorescent tubes used at concessions and in the bathrooms, and film reels.

"Two words," Mr. Peterson told them when he posted the note, pointing to the storage shelf. "Flammable." He counted on one finger. "Toxic." He counted on another. His mother said something about mercury in fluorescent lighting, too. She was a real nurse.

William felt for the light switch beside him and shot it up and down. He waited for the light, but it didn't come.

"Hello? Ma'am, are you in here?"

The darkness swelled.

"Shit."

A cold panic settled within him. The only reason to fear the dark, he reminded himself, was because of the unknown hidden within. His father had told him this. Identify the threat, he'd say.

But the actress was no threat to him. And he'd seen this room every day, all summer long.

Nothing to be afraid of.

So, why didn't the angst that dwelled within his every bone dissipate?

Because you're a fraidy cat.

His father's voice this time.

A wetness squelched beneath William's shoes as he, carefully, felt for a flashlight on the supply shelf. His hands found a thick roll of parking tickets. Good. He picked the right shelf. He reached to the left too quickly and sent aluminum cans crashing to the floor.

William startled. His pulse pounded behind his eyes and drummed in his ears. He tried again and finally found the metal handle of a flashlight. He sighed in relief and clicked it on. The floors were slick with a red goo and, before he knew it, William's long legs spilled out from beneath him with a quick squeak from his shoes. He threw his arms back to catch himself too late, and the crown of his head collided with the cement floor.

His flashlight pointed to the far corner of the room, where the door to the stairwell leading to the projection room was. He swung the light to the far end of the room, and William blinked away the disorientation swimming in his head. Still, he couldn't be sure if what he saw was real. It could be a gag. A conjuration of his state. A trick of the jitters. It was part of the show. Had to be.

The fair-skinned nurse hunched over the hefty man's unmoving body. William saw floating duplicates of both of them like when a cartoon character gets bashed over the head and sees stars. The nurse held two of the highly flammable projection rods. She twisted them, one at a time, like a corkscrew, into each of the man's eye sockets. Only he didn't react. He didn't scream. Or thrash.

William remembered how still the man had been as the nurse towed him away. No one was that good of an actor, right?

William lifted his head, still dizzy with pain.

This isn't real.

The nurse circled the man, admiring her work, and ignored William. Then, she leaned over the rods, resting both of her palms atop them, like she was thinking. She gripped each and twisted the rods deeper, through the eye and into the brain with a sound like beef thrown on a slab. The nurse, determined in her mutilation, gave the rods a final crank, cracking the back of the man's skull.

Why hadn't the man reacted? William had seen plenty of horror films and seen men scream for a lot less. That had to be agony. It nauseated him.

He didn't have much time to think about it. Before William knew it, the nurse was on him. She brought her strong hands around his throat. She dug her thumbs against the little ball in his neck. He gagged as he swallowed involuntarily, air restricted. He fought with all the resistance the dead man lacked. Without missing a beat, she beat William's head against the cement to quiet his fussing, but he fought on.

She dug deeper into his throat with her red thumb nails. Then, all at once. She stopped. William took the chance and pinned her onto her back.

His eyes burned into hers, and he didn't see the multi-legged creature slide out from beneath her. Didn't catch it skitter over to him. He only felt it once it had crept over his shoulder, and latched onto his spine.

The villainous nurse's eyes sobered into confusion. Then, horror. She brought her hands to William's wrists and tried to pull them free. But he tightened his grasp. "Please," she coughed.

But in that moment, William was gone. He lifted the nurse's head from the floor and pounded it back down. Again and again. Dousing him in her blood.

When there wasn't much left of her head, William tossed the nurse aside. She fell beside the dead man. He'd been dead all along, the creature mused.

It took its new host back outside into the lot. It would let the kid lead the way. For now, it sank back into the depths of William, and gave him back to the night as he left the storage room behind.

William winded around the side of the concession building and felt a heaviness in the back of his head, a headache coming on.

Floating, blurry lights guided him forward as the pain throbbed with persistence.

"Look who it is," a voice said. His vision focused on those bright red lips from earlier that evening.

When he didn't say anything, she tossed a cigarette into the mud and didn't bother stomping it out.

"Long time no see," Ingrid said.

William, shy as always, struggled for words. "How—" He had to think of something. Then he remembered the thunderous roar of laughter and the nurse. He wondered where she'd gone off to. Back to the show, he supposed. There it was. The show.

"How are you liking the show?" he asked.

He noticed the other girl, June, had been looking him up and down.

"What's that all over your shirt?"

Ingrid and William followed June's pointed finger to the splatters of crimson sinking into the white cotton.

William tugged the hem of his t-shirt, so he could see for himself. "Oh my god."

Panic struck him and he tried to recall an explanation.

The creature clicked its pincers and just as William shot a hand to his spine, it took control once more.

His arm fell awkwardly to his side. The creature searched William's consciousness and produced a response.

"Oh, just a bit I did for late comers."

His smile, uncertain and blushing before, turned sly. Too big for his face. Too wide to look sane.

Without another word, he walked right through June and Ingrid, separating them.

"William?" June called.

But he kept on toward Anna Lou's Chevy Bel Air.

There, the girl sat in the driver seat, primping, waiting for him.

In the reflection of the glass, he stared back at himself. A strange, emotionless gaze.

The door nearly hit him as it stretched open.

"Quit starin' at me," Anna Lou said, "and get in."

He did.

The usual RESTROOMS sign had been replaced with six white letters plastered over a black-painted wooden plaque. MORGUE it read, with an arrow directing patrons to either side. This got a laugh out of June.

Vomit bags lined the metal shelf beneath the large vanity in the ladies' room. A woman who looked about the same age as June's mother powdered the shiny ball of her nose. She did so absentmindedly, unblinking and entranced by her own reflection. She was as white as a sheet.

She and Ingrid made for the furthest stalls, surprised to see a few small children bustling around the cramped restroom with their mothers. They slid the door locks in place with twin *click*s.

The Tingler, June analyzed further, was a lot of fun, but plenty scary, too, especially if you read the papers. All that talk of nuclear energy, atomic bombs, and medical experiments–science that had the potential to or already had gone terribly wrong.

June couldn't blame the pale woman for responding to that film exactly as William Castle teased the audience might; with nausea, hysteria, and shock.

If viewers thought about it long enough, immersed themselves in the experience of film, they'd see these very *real* subjects like war in the horror movies they consumed. That alone was terrifying, never mind a parasite that feeds on fear like the Tingler.

Of course, this was the brilliance of the film, too.

June tried to think of things such as this instead of the china doll nurse and the dull bite of an emerging headache. The pair summoned bloody visions of her grandmother, and she did not want to go there.

June hummed an Elvis tune to herself. The bathroom was plenty loud enough, between the otherworldly swamp sounds like in *The Creature From The Black Lagoon* playing over the speakers and the crossover of conversations.

June dropped her poodle skirt, spotting a few stains from Officer Reed's masochistic and messy getaway. She couldn't stand that man, but was thankful for a distraction.

The music distorted into a shrill ring.

June's mouth went dry. She rubbed her tongue against the roof of her mouth and swallowed but found no relief. That's when she realized how heavy she was breathing. Furious and panicked shallow breaths escaped her lips. She hunched over as pain punched her skull. Tension shot through her neck and down her back like her spine was aflame. She gasped, bracing herself with her hands stretched to either side of the stall.

Women shuffled outside her door, bending to search for shoes of sitting women and girls, the indicator of occupancy. Through the space at the bottom of the stall door, June no longer saw the bathroom floor, but dirt. Bloody chunks of meat strewn within it. Eager carrion beetles swept over them. Was that a beak, from a bird or chicken? More dirt fell upon the mound, some tossed over onto June's own feet. She heard soft whimpers and then a squeal of terror. Something thrashed beneath the mound of dirt.

The edges of June's vision waned and soon became a storm of red smoke, except for the rattling box beneath the dirt. It ceased, and a fierce laughter and screams from what sounded like a dozen or more people ensued. Children, too.

The dirt settled, but June could hear the beetles. Crawling atop something solid, then gnawing away at something slick and gamey. Flesh.

A theatrically ghoulish voice, distant but sobering, said, "Ten minutes 'til showtime."

Anticipatory dread tormented her, coiling and springing in her gut. An agitated snake ready to strike. She thought she might retch. She cupped a hand over her mouth, and the voice repeated, "Ten minutes 'til showtime."

The red fog held its grasp on her.

We just saw The Tingler.

Next, Cat People.

This isn't real.

Immense pressure knotted in her throat, leaving her wheezing and prying at an invisible assailant's hands. The sense was taking control, filtering her out of her consciousness and into a sea of misery. She thought of Janice's broken ankle. Her grandmother's final moments. The boy she plowed over with a vehicle in her dreams. The soldiers overseas. What it was like to be shot. To starve.

Everyone was hurting; suffering was infinite.

She resisted with all her might. Trying to call herself back.

If June leaned too hard into the sense, she would feel it all. In strange circumstances, like earlier that week, she could see it, too. And if she stayed for too long, wandered too far, she feared she could be lost forever.

She felt a vibration against her lips. She'd begun humming the playful theme from *The Blob*, again.

She focused and visualized the clouds of red floating away and returning to the moment.

Focus.

Ingrid's hand shot from under the shared wall between them and toward June's feet. "Hey, Junie, you got one?"

When June didn't answer, Ingrid knocked on the shared wall. The noise rang in June's head, thunderous and booming. She turned toward the sound and saw her grandmother once more. She smiled, then her head swung back with a *crack*. When it came up and faced June, it was someone else. A man. Face smashed to a pulp. She brought her head forward and into her hands.

Focus.

"June?"

A young boy, accompanied by his mother, took a spill on the floor, getting a good bump on his head and erupted into hysterics. Was that what June sensed? Is that why pain prodded around in her skull?

The boy screamed and June hugged herself and rocked.

This can't be happening. This can't be happening.

"Shhh," a woman, the mother perhaps, said. "It's alright. Where does it hurt?"

As if the mother spoke to her, June indicated the specific spot just beneath the crown of her head by bringing a hand to it. It throbbed under her hand.

"Here," June said.

Ingrid waved her hand, searching the air for a tampon. "Where is it, June?"

"Here," June repeated, touching a slightly lower position on her head.

The boy's wailing eased, and so did the blinding red before June. He sniffled.

"I feel a little bump," the mother said. "We'll get some ice on it, but I think you'll live."

The pair shuffled out of the restroom, which fell as quiet as a morgue after hours.

"June?" Ingrid said with a degree of impatience.

June saw Ingrid's waving hand and bent wrist, coming to.

"Oh." June unwound toilet paper and passed it beneath the stall, her hand brushing Ingrid's.

All at once, the red lifted completely.

"No, June," Ingrid said, exasperated. "You know what I mean."

Finally, June did. June was the group's tampon supplier. Most mothers in town bought into the whole tampons robbing young girls of their virginity hysterics.

Not June's.

She passed the tampon.

"*THANK YOU.*"

June wondered how long her friend had been waiting on her, speaking to her. Ingrid's toilet flushed and June sat up, shaking away the remaining disorientation. She flushed her own toilet only for the reassurance of reality. A sign that she was rooted back in herself.

"You doing okay?" Ingrid asked as she and June exited their stalls. The doors groaned as they swung on their hinges.

"Yes. Sorry, I was miles away for a second."

"I don't think anyone could blame you after the week you've had," Ingrid said.

Ingrid scrubbed her hands as June hunched over the sink. She rocked on her heels.

"June?"

The red had vanished, but the throbbing had not. She felt another strike against the back of her head.

"Just a headache."

Ingrid hurried for paper towels and the wind of her movement sent green vomit bags floating from the vanity's ledge. They fell to the floor and stuck in the strange wetness floors of public restrooms always had.

Ingrid ran the paper towel under cold water and moved June's ponytail over her shoulder. June's skin prickled.

Upon the cool contact, June felt relief. Ingrid took it away and held it to June's forehead, then over each eye. As if it were a dying bulb, the pain dissipated. June turned her head from side to side, awaiting the painful impact, but it was gone. Just like that. It was like she'd just come back from another world. Back from the dead.

"Better?"

June nodded.

"Good. Let's go see the show, then. And get some water in you before you have more popcorn."

Ingrid tossed the damp paper towel into the trash bin positioned near the door.

Blood returned to June's face and the dizziness died down.

Ingrid lit a cigarette, eyes narrowing, inspecting her friend for something.

"Thanks for taking such good care of me."

Ingrid winked. "You get feeling bad again, you tell me, okay?"

The cigarette wagged between her lips with each word she spoke. This always made June smile.

"I'll be fine."

"Let me help you. A lot's happened, June."

June wasn't sure anyone could really help her. Help distract her? Maybe. Help ease some of the pain? Apparently.

"And if there's anything you want to talk about, I'm here."

June smiled. "Thanks, Ingrid."

She didn't say more, though she suspected Ingrid was hoping for it. June just wanted to enjoy the rest of the night. It was senior year, and for all they knew, it could be their last summer at the drive-in.

June hurried past Ingrid, catching her arm. "Let's go find the guys."

Just as they left the restroom, they spotted the shy blonde kid from the ticket booth. The pastor's son. William.

Ingrid spoke to him, but June stared into his eyes. There was something behind them. Something pleading and desperate. She'd catch it and then it was gone again. She dismissed it, smiling politely. She'd just had an ordeal. Her brain was still adjusting.

Stand down, she thought.

Then, she noticed the blood on his shirt.

CHAPTER
TEN

Friday, August 7, 1959

9:07 PM

The creature let the boy rise to the surface and lead the conversation with the girl. It could tap in and out of control, relinquish and retake it as it pleased. It wasn't at full strength, not yet fully realized, though it would be soon.

The creature felt more acquainted with humans the longer it latched onto its host. The more fear it stirred in them, the stronger its hatred became. That particular human—William, others called it—harbored a primal fear that radiated. It was so powerful. So warm. The creature considered snapping his neck then and there.

All in due time.

It thrived in chaos, renewed its power in carnage.

The creature had to be patient. In patience lay its identity. Its ultimate revival.

William was groggy. His thoughts were distant and dull, like he'd been under sedation. He'd awoken to a beam so bright he put a hand up to shield his eyes. He turned and was surprised to be inside the Bel Air with Anna Lou. How did he get there, he wondered.

A presence shrouded over him. Looming and grim. His chest rose and fell in quick succession. He hesitated a moment, then he peaked over his shoulder and checked the backseat.

It was empty.

Anna Lou watched the large black panther circle its cage on screen. She loved Jacques Tourneur's *Night of the Demon,* so she was eager to see one of the director's earlier films.

William absorbed this detail as Anna spoke, but it seemed distant, like something someone else observed for him and re-layed the message.

"Anyway," Anna Lou said, waving her arms as if she'd said too much. "Mind turning it up a bit?"

William hadn't noticed the speaker clipped to his window. He twisted the volume knob, discovering a crusty substance pilling on his fingers.

Anna Lou grabbed a dusty rag from the dashboard and of-fered it to him.

"Sorry, it's all I have." She gave him a once over. "For the blood," she said.

He remembered running into Ingrid and June then.

"What's all over your shirt?" June had asked.

William brought his ungainly arms out before him. He flipped his palms up, then down. A dark wetness spotted him in places and spattered in others. It cracked with itchiness as it dried, like it had on his fingers. He scratched a bit of it away from his elbow, and it clotted beneath his nails.

It smelled metallic. Like copper or iron.

Where had the blood come from?

"Bet it's fun to be part of the show," Anna Lou said.

"What?" William saw Anna Lou's pink lips moving, but he was hearing something else. A part of him arguing with an invisible force.

Let go, he thought.

Leave me alone.

Where had that come from?

Anna Lou couldn't have made him feel such disdain. She was lovely, even if she did make him nervous as hell. Her freckled face was sweet with a kindness that never went dull, even when she wasn't smiling. At least with him, anyway. He thought she'd be great in one of those black and white crime films. Noir, they called it.

So, what was it then? Why did every nerve within him scream for him to look behind himself again and again?

"What're you thinking about?" Anna Lou asked, following his eyes to the backseat, then the rear window. She smoothed her skirt across her knees and tucked her hands beneath her. "Still in murder mode? If you're in on any more tricks, you count me out. Do you hear me?"

Her eyes pointed an accusatory glare at the blood. He looked down. How did he not know where it came from? Why didn't he remember how it got there?

What did it matter? It was obviously fake. Had to be. What was it filmmakers used for blood in pictures? Chocolate sauce, red dye, and corn syrup? It had to be that. Though it didn't have that cartoonishly bright red color shown in horror movies like *The Tingler*. And there was the smell . . .

Itchy flares broke out across his flesh. He leapt from his seat, skin crawling. A tight pinch between his shoulder blades made him gasp.

"Whoa," Anna Lou said, giggling.

"I think I'm allergic to the stuff," William said. He clawed at his neck, hands, and forearms in a frenzy. It was like his body had become a new home for fire ants.

Let go.

Let me go.

"Can't make it in Hollywood, then." She stuck her tongue out at him. "Sorry, kid."

He laughed, the sound startling himself.

The itch spread down his back and he reached to scratch. Before he could, the creature wormed into position and sank its pincers into his neck. His laughter crescendoed, more maniacal. Mad. And terrifying. Tears sprang from his eyes with hiccuping sobs. Then, he laughed again. Louder. With more malevolence.

"Stop that." Anna Lou crossed her arms.

Anna Lou tried for defiance, but the creature knew she was afraid. It could feel it. Saliva flooded William's mouth, dripped over his bottom lip, and onto the seat. He threw his head up, veins stretched and taut around his neck like a noose.

"William? Are you alright?"

A woman onscreen warned of black cats and an accompanying curse. The light shifts onscreen flashed across William's deranged smile.

"Stop it," Anna Lou said. She gave him a good shove and her popcorn bucket fell to the floor. "Now you've done it."

She sighed and scooped the popcorn into the bucket. "I told you we have to keep the car clean or Daddy will never let me take it out again."

She found him still transfixed on her, still wearing that all-wrong, too-wide grin. A crooked imitation of the boy's otherwise kind face.

"William, stop it. You're frightening me," Anna Lou said.

The creature slinked its body up and down with eagerness, dancing along the boy's scrawny spine. This kill was ready to be devoured. It was trembling.

The creature guided its host and it snatched at Anna Lou. She hurried away, pinning herself to the door.

"Stop it!" she demanded.

The creature reached once more and its host fell into the bench, face down. The creature whipped its host back up in a swift inhuman motion, as if the torso and limbs were disjointed.

"Get out, William! Get out!"

She screamed a beautiful, horrified screech. The creature squirmed with pleasure.

The humans wouldn't be alarmed if they heard her cries. It didn't have to kill deep within the woods anymore. Or in the quiet of a storage room. The humans screamed at this place, encouraging one another to. Booming voices from all directions demanded it with a note of crackling static behind it. These humans sought terror, but assumed safety. The creature thought of no better place it could be.

Anna Lou tried for the door, and the creature shot its strength through its host's limbs. It lifted and flipped the girl into the backseat. Her eyes indicated surprise at the thin kid's newfound strength. She landed hard against the leather. It was good to disorient the kill, the creature knew. It was another means of controlling it.

She swung at the creature's host. He grabbed her wrists with such force that she winced and yelped.

"William," she sobbed. "Stop!"

The creature savored the girl's disbelief. This wasn't supposed to happen. Not to her and not with this boy. But the boy would soon be swimming in spilled blood. They all would.

Anna Lou rammed her knee between the host's legs and he released her. She climbed up to the rearview window and screamed, pounding into the glass. The creature clasped a hand over her mouth, infuriated. She tried to bite at the host, but as her jaws expanded, the creature stuffed the host's pocketed vomit bags into her mouth. One after the other. She struggled against him, and with each cry came a strangled cough. Gagging. The creature crammed more of the green plastic down her throat and cupped his hand firm over her mouth.

Her legs kicked and kicked, but it was no use. The host was too strong with the creature tacked onto its spine. At that point, the boy was more monster than man.

In a final effort, Anna Lou reached a hand to William's face. He turned away from her, but she kept coming at him. Grabbing at anything she could get a hold of. She found his eye and jammed her thumb into it. William didn't so much as howl despite the spray of fluid that expelled from the socket and onto her.

Soon, the thrashing slowed to a stop. Bubbly yellow fluid bubbled from the girl's mouth as her head lolled into the seat. Vomit bags, ripped to shreds and half-digested lay across her tongue and down her throat.

The creature was satisfied.

CHAPTER ELEVEN

Friday, August 7, 1959
9:14 PM

Arthur ended up staying with Lenny and Stef for the second film. June suspected it was due to Stef's stash of cotton candy. Arthur always had a sweet tooth after he'd smoked. She, Ingrid, and Vincent sat in the Studebaker watching one of the most famous scenes in *Cat People*.

It was Vincent's first time watching it. He held the popcorn bucket in his lap, mindlessly munching as Alice walked the dark street, heels clicking against the pavement. Hands in pocket, Alice moved in and out of shadows, without music. A perfect setup for the scare to come.

Hiss.

Vincent jumped from his seat, sending popcorn over the front bench.

"Watch it," Ingrid said, catching a few pieces in her hand. She tossed them into her mouth.

Stef squealed from the truck beside them.

Ingrid rolled her eyes and pointed to Vincent's truck. "You could scare that one with a kitten."

June turned to face Vincent in the backseat. He was sweating. "They got ya." June stuck her tongue out at him. "It's fun, right?"

Vincent shook his head, readjusting the popcorn bucket in his lap. June grabbed it from him.

"It wasn't that scary," he shrugged.

Ingrid snorted beside June.

"You sure looked scared," June teased.

Ingrid waved a hand as new images blinked onto the screen. "Alright, you two. Pipe down. I'm trying to watch the show."

June crossed her legs beneath her, adjusting her skirt around her knees.

She licked her fingers clean of butter and passed the bucket to Ingrid, who pulled a cigarette away from her lips to eat and slurp her soda.

June liked the way the smoke curled around and framed Ingrid's face. She didn't bother blowing it out the window with Vincent lighting 'em up in the back.

"You're right, June," Ingrid said. "*Cat People* is a good one."

"I tried telling you," June said.

What June liked most about *Cat People* was its use of shadows. Unlike most horror movies, Tourneur's film never *really* showed the scares. Instead, the director used sounds and shadows to suggest to the audience impending doom, transformations, murder, and even death. And it was effective.

The woman who played Irena, Simone Simon, was great despite what others said of her. Hollywood tabloids called her "temperamental" and "abrasive."

June knew it wasn't difficult to be labeled a *temperamental* or *hysteric* or *crazy* woman. Like the men of Salem who accused women of witchcraft for simply disagreeing with or rejecting them, modern men were quick to cry hysteria the moment women expressed concern or passion for just about anything. And that's what June saw in *Cat People* and all the other films where a woman warned of the monster or villain. AND THE WOMEN, like Irena warning of the curse, WERE RIGHT ALL ALONG!

Razor-sharp claws slashed toward the audience onscreen.

The audience responded with cries of terror. But June heard one, not too far away, that was blood-curdling. There was no humor within it, just sheer horror.

Tourneur was good, but he wasn't that good. Plus, the picture was nearly twenty years old. June had seen far scarier stuff, like falling into a boiling vat of wax in *House of Wax*.

Why then, did her heart feel like it was going to leap from within her chest, through blood and bone and flesh?

The scream came again. Too real. Too urgent. It reverberated through her skull, down her spine, and through each limb. She jerked in her seat. The others didn't take notice.

She listened again for the heinous cry, but it had died away.

June swallowed a sip of her soda and something like plastic crawled over her tongue and down her throat. She coughed against it, feeling a lurch in her stomach.

She wanted to get through the night. She took another sip and reached for the volume control knob and cranked it up. The pictures were supposed to be loud, anyway. They were at the theater.

Her friends exchanged glances but didn't complain.

She saw Arthur leave the truck, a cigarette between his lips. He wore a sly smile. He was on the hunt for some backseat bingo. A panther's roar erupted from the lot's speakers and June shot her eyes to the screen.

When she checked out the window once more, Arthur was gone. Part of her wanted to follow him. Get him back to the truck because— *What? Because you think you heard a scream at a horror show?*

June returned her attention to the screen. She tried to hone in on Tourneur's every tactic, every detail utilized to add to the atmosphere of the film, and not that of her own reality. Because her reality was fine. She was fine.

Everyone is fine.

Lenny called from the truck. "Hey, a little help. I think Stef has fainted."

June didn't have to be asked twice. She took the distraction and dashed to the truck. She opened the rickety driver's side door and saw sweet Stef hunched over the dash. Ingrid was on June's heels, followed by Vincent.

"What happened?" June asked.

Lenny shook his head. "She was doing fine with this film, I swear. I would've told her to look away if it got too scary. But it must've been and she got herself worked up before I knew it."

It wasn't that. Lenny was a good guy, the best of them, maybe, but he was male. And men always assessed women's health and distress with scrutiny of their emotions. Ingrid's eyes met June's, narrow with concern, indicating she felt the same way. It wasn't the movie.

"Had she eaten?" Ingrid asked June and Lenny.

Lenny showed an empty popcorn bucket and candy wrappers. So, she shouldn't have been lightheaded from hunger.

Lenny spoke in mumbles, stopped, and began again. He failed to string anything comprehensible together, and his brow knitted, and his teeth dug into his bottom lip. A prick of pain found June's own lip, though her teeth remained in her mouth.

She paused. Lenny met her gaze, and that's when June saw the fear on his face. He'd said the wrong thing, but he was worried for Stef. But something else rattled him, too.

"We have to wake her up before he comes back."

He, as in Officer Reed.

June and Ingrid understood. They nodded.

"Lenny, I love ya," Ingrid said, "but get outta the way and let me and June in."

Ingrid and June climbed into the truck and Vincent stood at the open window.

"Stef?" Ingrid asked. "Stef, wake up."

"I've tried that," Lenny said with a bite.

Stef remained slouched and still.

Ingrid moved red strands of hair from Stef's face and tucked them behind her ear.

"Stef?" Ingrid tried once more. Nothing. "June, hand me her soda."

June did, and Ingrid snatched it away. She threw out the straw and lid and dove her hand into the soda, splashing it on the seats and a little on June, too. Ingrid cupped dripping ice in her hand.

"Lay her back," Ingrid said, and June did so. Lenny climbed to the middle of the backseat to support Stef's head.

"Is she—"

You would've thought they were injecting Stef with the world's thickest needle.

"Shush," Ingrid said. She took one piece of ice and traced the curves of Stef's face. Around her forehead, down the bridge of her nose. Stef would not be happy about her ruined blush. Water streaked through it. When the ice melted to slosh, Ingrid shook it free of her hand, sending a light spray over Vincent.

Ingrid dug for more ice, her hand bright red from the cold.

"Lift her head," Ingrid ordered Lenny. He did, and she slapped ice on the back of her friend's neck. She hoped the shock of it would awaken Stef.

It did.

Stef gasped. Her eyes fluttered and her head lulled as she came to, but Lenny's hands were there to guide her.

"No! Let me go!" Stef cried.

Lenny let go, sending Stef's head back in a way that June knew would make her friend's neck ache later.

"It's just Lenny," Ingrid reasoned. She brought Stef's hands into her own. "It's okay. It's us."

Stef's eyes circled around the group.

Her legs shook. Her hands trembled. "Where is he?"

"Who?" Vincent asked.

Stef began to cry.

"Who?" Lenny echoed. "What's wrong?"

Ingrid and June both rubbed their palms in soothing circles across Stef's back.

Finally, between heaving sobs, she blubbered, "William."

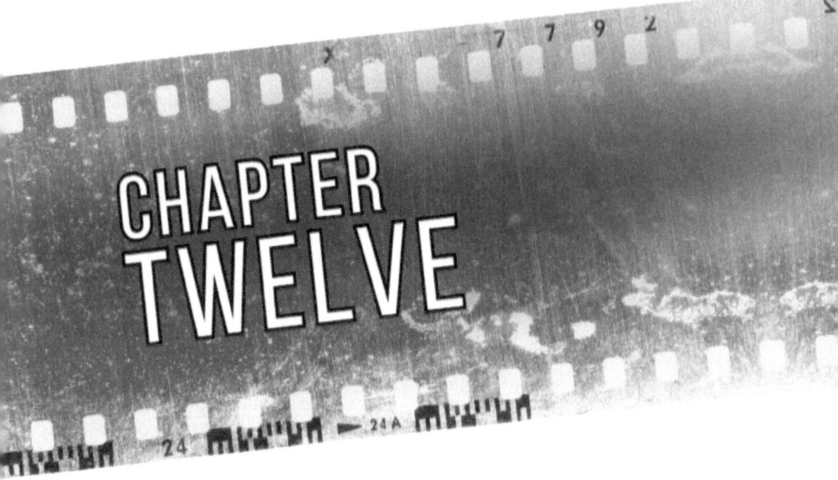

CHAPTER TWELVE

They'd missed the rest of *Cat People*, but June didn't care. She felt in her bones that whatever her friend saw was real. Something had been eating at her all night. She thought of the beetles, the mounding dirt that she'd seen in the restroom. The pounding from beneath it. That vision had felt different, somehow.

And that mattered, she decided.

Ingrid played her nurse role better than the actresses stationed around the Peterson's Pictures Drive-In lot. June knew herself that even in her touch, her casual words, there was something nurturing in Ingrid, no matter how tough she was.

So, while she cared for Stef and revived her back into coherence, June prodded.

"Stef," June took in a deep breath, hoping Stef would do the same. She did, and they exhaled together. Their eyes met. "Tell us what you saw."

Lenny sat up, attentive.

On the screen, Irena lay just outside the zoo's caged panther. Then, the credits rolled.

The ghoulish showman boomed over the lot's speakers. "How about that one, folks?"

The audience cheered and rooted from their cars, clapping.

Panthers roared over the sound system.

"Next up is *Shock*, starring who?"

A recognizable and deep menacing laugh followed the announcer. He continued, "You guessed it! Vincent Price in his *very* first starring role."

Shock was the film June had been most looking forward to, but right now nothing mattered more than Stef.

"Okay, Stef," Ingrid said. "Feel like sipping a Coke or nibbling on some candy?"

Lenny offered a small pouch of milk chocolate candies. Stef shoved it away.

"Listen to me!" Stef shouted. The sudden burst of energy startled them all.

Lenny and Vincent exchanged a glance.

Stef shuddered a breath and raised a shaking hand. "William was in that red car." She pointed to Annie's Chevy Bel-Air that sat two rows ahead diagonally, its driver side door ajar. Their eyes followed. "The car was shaking, so I assumed they were, well, you know."

They did. The group nodded. Vincent had a small grin that Lenny extinguished when he smacked his palm into the back of his friend's head.

"And?" June said.

"And, I saw Annie *clawing* at the backseat. Like she was trying to get out."

Stef sniffled.

"She was so scared. I've never seen someone so afraid."

June knew something hadn't felt right, and here it was, the proof that she wasn't suffering from lunacy or being hysterical.

June rested a hand on Stef's jittering shoulder.

"That's when I saw William come from behind her and pull her back. He had his hand around her throat," Stef continued through sobs.

The open driver side door bothered June.

"Did you see William leave the car?" she asked.

Stef shook her head. "I must've fainted by then."

"I'm going to go check it out," June said. "Vincent, you coming?"

Lenny sat up, ready to help. "I am, too."

"No," Stef said, turning to stop him. "We can't let Officer Reed see you leave the truck."

Vincent offered an apologetic frown. "She's right. You stay with Stef and Ingrid. Hold down the fort. We'll be right back."

Just as Vincent and June left the vehicle, the concession lights were cut. Despite the late hour, the air remained sticky. The wind was light and did nothing to dispel the oppressive weight of the humidity.

When they were out of the gang's earshot, Vincent said, "I don't know what Stef saw, but I think Annie could take that scrawny boy."

June stopped. It was a valid point, but June believed her friend. Trusted the disturbance she'd felt.

"Stef isn't making it up."

Vincent hushed. They weaved their way through vehicles. Cicadas sang their droning summer song, and aside from chattering moviegoers, the lot was quiet.

Just then, a cluster of human-shaped shadows emerged from behind the concession stands and past the Studebaker and truck. Barefooted and in hospital gowns, "patients" moaned as they trudged through the thick mud.

"Time for your medicine," one man said, moaning afterwards as if he'd received a painful injection.

A group of nearby teens squealed.

"The doctor's in," said another man at least twenty years older than them.

A man reached into a '98 Oldsmobile and shouted at a startled couple. "I saw lights in the sky. They're here. From the beyond."

He repeated it, urging them to believe him.

"Go, while you still can!"

The other actors roamed through the lot, swatting at invisible pests or rolling their head from one shoulder to the other, mouths hanging open.

June and Vincent crept up to the Bel Air's rear and saw no immediate sign of occupancy. June rounded for the passenger side and knocked on the window before she cupped her eyes and leaned in for a peak. Popcorn and green vomit bags were scattered over the bright red and white seating. As far as June could tell, no one was inside.

Just as she pressed off the glass window, June was struck with a hammering sensation in her joints, like every part of her was bruised, throbbing with blood. Then, the pain climbed to her skull, nesting there. She tried not to react too violently in case Stef was still watching.

The projector resurrected its bright glow—the perfect spotlight on the unoccupied vehicle.

She wanted to inspect further. She made for the driver side of the vehicle, but as she passed the trunk, something grabbed ahold of her ankle.

She shrieked and jumped back.

A man appeared, clawing through the mud.

"It's time for your medicine!"

He gnashed his teeth at her while another psychiatric patient reached for Vincent, sending him backing away on his heels.

The man who grabbed June surfaced. His mud-slicked hospital gown gave him an even more disheveled appearance. He slammed the Bel-Air's open door with a ferocious growl like a bloodthirsty werewolf.

A teen two cars over with a cigarette between his lips tossed it without stomping the butt and dove back into his car after an actor stopped and stared at him with wicked intent.

June and Vincent hurried back toward the truck. They scurried around a limping man who repeated under his breath and to no one in particular, "Time for your evaluation."

This struck June. She'd come out on the lot because she believed her friend. Because Stef had validated the growing disturbance within her.

Something screamed within her and told her to act faster. Confront the disturbance, the inevitable pain. Something had happened in that car. She knew it.

Screams erupted across the lot. Several well-rehearsed, others natural and unsettling. Like only some of the crowd was in on the joke.

The screams unnerved her. She looked around the group and remembered Arthur was gone.

"Vincent, we have to find Arthur."

The showman returned to the speakers. "Don't be alarmed. Remain in your vehicles. We've contacted authorities."

A mechanical police siren and red light ascended from the middle of the lot.

It was Officer Reed.

Vincent was making his way back to the truck.

"We have to find Arthur," she repeated, with a grittier edge than before.

Vincent sighed. "June. It's just a show. It's the show that's got Stef spooked. And Arthur can handle himself."

"It's not just a show anymore," June argued. There was fear beneath her fury, and the next thing she said came out more desperately than she understood herself. "We need to find him now."

CHAPTER THIRTEEN

Friday, August 7, 1959
10:11 PM

The creature sensed a change in its host. Its own perception through William's eyes tunneled on one side. A consequence of the girl jamming her thumb into it. But that wasn't the only change. William grew restless under the creature's control.

I want to go home. Please, let me go.

Hot tears slid from the boy's good eye, along with a pungent smell of pus from the other one. The creature recognized the scent and worried about infection. The wound needed tending to. But the wound wasn't its own. It knew that. Yet it had the sudden urge to treat it. It even had this newfound knowledge of how to do so, which it assumed came from the host.

Even in the grip of death, humans made plans to save themselves. Futile and ignorant.

Please let me go. Please.

Though the voice remained in the birth canal of thought and didn't reach William's lips, it was loud for the creature. It thwacked against its host's spine, straightening it out, quieting it down.

With brute force, the creature guided William to the edge of the lot. There stood a kid with his back to William. He was far taller and stronger than William, but not William's host, of course. A name broke the host's repressed conscience, **ARTHUR.**

"Oh, come on," Arthur said to the blonde nurse. "You call it a night and come with me."

The nurse stretched her arms before her as though she was reaching for Arthur, ready to nab him. She groaned like the living dead. He was undeterred.

"We would have a truck all to ourselves," he said, smoothing a hand over the curls above his ear.

With a series of glances over her shoulder, the nurse recruited fellow *patients* to scare him off.

Arthur's bravado faltered, and he brought his hands up in defense. "Easy."

The beings came upon him waving at imaginary flies and annoyances. Another muttered something about the doctor poisoning him. "And they'll poison you, too!" That actor jabbed a finger at the center of Arthur's chest. The others formed around him, growling and jeering. The headlights of the vehicles created a perfect stage for the actors and Arthur. Their passengers cheered, and others gasped. Arthur backed further from the lot and into the dark veil of the trees.

The creature crept forward, just at the edge of the light, just enough so only those closest could see its host's face. The blonde nurse noticed William's injury. Her expression contorted into one of terror.

Arthur followed her gaze over his shoulder. He hadn't seen William circling him. He sucked air through his teeth and laughed. "Shit, man," he said, meeting William and bringing a hand to his shoulder. "You got me, good."

When William didn't respond, Arthur removed his hand. An awkward and unsettling air hung between them.

A few actors climbed into the hearse beneath the screen, occasionally poking their distraught or expressionless faces from behind the curtain windows and to the glass. Others returned to the rear of the lot like monsters hidden in the dark.

The creature hummed within as it sensed the burning warmth radiating from Arthur, who appeared more suspicious by the second.

"Hey, William," Arthur said, incredulous. He pointed to William's injured eye and hissed. "That looks bad."

William feigned a smile, but Arthur's repulsion was unmistakable. Something clicked. The creature could see it all over his face. It was how the dark-haired nurse had looked when the creature found her, right before she'd begun to understand that she'd been targeted by something wicked.

The opening credits of *Shock* rolled on screen.

Arthur turned to the glow of the projector.

He looked back to William, who had come much closer. Sneering. He stepped forward.

Arthur bolted, spooked.

And the creature chased that terror with absolute delight.

Friday, August 7, 1959
10:27 PM

"**D**o not be alarmed!" a voice came over the speakers throughout the lot. "Ladies and gentlemen, psychiatric patients have escaped the hospital. Please, remain in your vehicles."

The film rolled as June and Vincent searched the lot for Arthur. They started with concessions, though the showman's demands left it mostly abandoned. Still, they thought he might go there to smoke.

Bored concession workers leaned against the counters, waiting for their shifts to end. June waited just outside the men's restroom as Vincent checked for Arthur there.

He came out shaking his head. "Nope."

"Where could he have gone?" June said, giving herself whiplash as she searched the lot. A fuse of panic ignited within her because there was no sign of William either. And if he did what Stef accused him of . . . She wanted her friend to be wrong more than anything, but she couldn't deny the swelling angst hammering in her chest, pounding like a fist in her ears.

The pain returned in her skull, and she let it steer her away from the lot and toward the dirt path, the only way in or out of the lot. Ahead was the tall ghostly glow of the Peterson's Pictures sign and marquee.

An invisible fist collided into June's face. She fell, muddying the knees of her skirt. The wet earth caked between her fingers, preserving her fallen hands in the ruts beside messy tire tracks.

"June? What's going on?"

Vincent rested his hands on June's shoulders, steadying her. He helped her to her feet. She shooed him away.

"He's in trouble," June said. She didn't think of Vincent or Lenny or Ingrid or Stef at that moment. The guiding inner voice gave her only one name, Arthur. She quickened her clumsy strides.

Vincent was on her heels. His work boots squelched through puddles.

As June ran, a part of herself split away, leaving her frantic body behind. She still saw the marquee, though she stood at the top. Out of body like she'd been as she watched her grandmother die. With a hand that wasn't her own, June swung at something in the shadow. It was a person. They spit blood, and the killer jerked their head forward. Though his eyes, nose, and lips were swollen three times their size, June knew who it was. The killer wound a rope around Arthur's throat. Around and around again. Through the killer's eyes, June watched as they secured the other end of the rope around the rail. She felt the bite of the frayed material in her hand.

Then, as she'd seen the intruder do to her grandmother, June outstretched her arms, connecting with the center of Arthur's chest. He tumbled over the rail. The bruising she'd felt burst alive in a pain so hot and renewed, it took her breath away. Air rushed over her from head to toe. The rope creaked as it was pulled taut.

Vincent grabbed June's hand, yanking her along as she returned to the moment.

When she came to, she said, "He's at the marquee."

Ahead of them, a shadow fell from the marquee. It thrashed in the moonlight.

June and Vincent reached the bottom of the marquee, and she screamed. Vincent stopped dead in his tracks. Arthur hung over their heads, dangling from the marquee on a rope. He struggled a final moment, twitched, and then stilled. His body was bathed in a cinematic golden glow as it slowly swung in the wicked wind.

Vincent jumped at his friend's feet like a helpless child. Arthur was out of reach. And he was already dead.

William stood above them, looking down at Arthur.

Vincent growled in fury and started towards the ladder. Without a moment's hesitation, William moved to the top of the ladder of the Peterson's Pictures sign and dove head first, into the woods. They heard heavy thuds as William's body collided with the strong oak trees on its way down.

They dashed into the woods after William and found his broken body where he'd landed.

His limbs were bent and horrifically jagged with broken bones. His neck was stuck to his right shoulder, exposing the kinks and knots of his fractured spine.

Vincent turned from the gore and bent over heaving, on the verge of vomiting.

June couldn't tear her eyes away from the body, and she saw a rustling in the brush beside William as something hurried away and disappeared further into the woods.

June gasped but couldn't fully trust that she saw anything. The shock of it all was like an endless ringing in her ears, vibrating through her body.

Vincent finally threw up, his whole body riddled with getting *the bad* out. He lurched forward and spit into the woods. He wiped his mouth, and when his eyes met June's, she felt a pang of agony.

She wept and said, "We have to get help. Let the police know that there are people actually dead here."

He nodded, swiping at tears.

They set out for the lot, for Officer Reed, without speaking a word.

When they reached the marquee, Ingrid, Stef, and Lenny ran up to them.

"We saw you guys take off," Lenny explained. He stopped and looked his friends over. "Are you guys okay?"

Vincent shook his head.

"We went to find Arthur," June managed. She looked at her friends, knowing she'd never be ready to deliver the news she had to. A few steps closer and they'd see Arthur hanging there.

"Stef was right," Vincent said.

Everyone looked at Stef.

"You mean about William?" she asked, nerves shaking each word through quivering lips.

June didn't know how else to say it, so she just did.

"William killed Arthur."

Their confusion was a way of the mind protecting itself, she thought. For they didn't appear immediately devastated.

"She's telling the truth," Vincent said, zipping through the words as if he was still running.

"How?" Ingrid asked. She came to June's side and saw it for herself.

Then the others did, too.

Lenny caught Stef as she screamed a devastated cry.

June said, "We have to find Officer Reed. Stef was right. William's dead, too."

Ingrid gasped. "What do you mean?"

"He threw himself from the marquee and into the woods," Vincent said.

Before he could elaborate any further, headlights found them.

June squinted and could see just enough of the body of the Ford 300 and its tail fins. It was Officer Reed. She ran towards his driver's side window.

Officer Reed's shoulder rose and fell as he cranked the window down.

"Leonard Raye, I do believe you've found yourself out of bounds."

"Officer Reed, come quick," she said. "Our friend's been killed."

"That's not something to joke about," Officer Reed said through the open window.

"It's true," June and the others pleaded.

Officer Reed swung his door open. June stepped back so it wouldn't collide into her.

He planted a black cowboy boot in the mud. "Ah," he complained, kicking his boot against the side of the car. June hurried back to the huddle.

"Look!" June yelled at him, pointing to their dangling friend, who twisted in slow circles back and forth. Back and forth. Rope creaking.

Then he saw it. June sensed his confusion. He took sharp and short inhales, and after a good look at the hanging, battered boy, looked away. June knew he was asking himself the same question they all had—*Is this real?*

How could it be?

"What," Officer Reed paused, caught his breath, and tried again. "What happened to him?"

For once, he didn't sound accusatory. He sounded like an adult taking action. There was hope for them yet.

"William got the rope around his neck and shoved him over the ledge," Vincent said.

"William? The preacher's boy?" he asked.

Vincent nodded. "Then he jumped from the ladder and killed himself. The body's in there." Vincent pointed to the break in the trees where he and June had entered.

Officer Reed circled the flashlight over their faces.

"Is anyone else hurt?" he asked.

"Maybe," Stef said, breaking away from Lenny. "Annie."

"The doc's daughter?" Officer Reed asked.

Stef nodded profusely. "We saw William attacking her in her car. It's parked in the lot."

"We didn't find her in it, though," June clarified.

Officer Reed thought on this, clearly trying to determine a course of action. This incident couldn't have been like anything he'd dealt with before. Crimes in their little town were never so heinous. Some recent burglaries, sure. Until her grandmother's death, people thought murder was for the pictures.

And then there's everything that's happened tonight.

"Stay here," Officer Reed commanded. "Make sure no one touches anything."

"Where are you going?" June asked.

"I have to find a call box or a telephone somewhere."

Officer Reed turned, but only his upper half responded. His feet stood firm in place. He reached down and tried to pull one of his legs free as if his foot was sunken and couldn't move. That didn't work either. As much as he fought, it was like his brain no longer operated his own limbs. Something else did. He grunted, straining his immobile limbs. Thick veins spread across his neck.

"What's happening?" Officer Reed shouted.

Officer Reed squirmed but remained planted. His arms convulsed in violent thrashes. Then, all too quickly, he fell still.

"Officer Reed?" June tried.

His head shot to his right shoulder. Then to the left. And in a quick whip like a cowboy, he spun his .38 revolver into his mouth and fired.

The teens screamed and soon after, the audience a short ways away did the same.

Something fell from Officer Reed's neck, landing on its back.

Ingrid cringed. "What is that?" she cried.

June couldn't believe her eyes. It was a massive insect, the size of a bread loaf, like something straight out of a monster movie. She stepped closer, inquisitive. Lenny's outstretched arm stopped her.

"Nobody go near it," he said.

The creature struggled as its furiously wiggling legs doubled in size.

"Oh my god," Stef said.

The creature righted itself, its body expanding every which way, its pincers grabbing toward them.

The gang stepped back, awe-struck with the horror of the thing before them.

It didn't feel real. It was too shocking and nightmarish to be true, but there was the dead policeman to remind them, *this is happening.*

The creature wriggled to face June, clicking its pincers. She froze like an animal that heard the unmistakable footfalls of a predator.

June thought about running. The creature would chase her away from her friends. Then they'd be safe to run. But what if she took off and they followed? She imagined those pincers gripping one of their ankles, climbing to their neck. Tossing their bodies from heights.

Without warning, the creature hurried toward the path and scurried across into the woods on the other side, behind the projector.

"What the hell was that?" Ingrid exclaimed. She held a hand over her heart and stomped in the mud.

Stef's alarmed face asked the same question.

"I saw something. That thing I think," June said, "when we found William."

"You mean that's what made William do that—" Lenny paused, his eyes wandering to their friend's hanged body. "—to Arthur?"

June's eyes followed his gaze.

She remembered the rope in her hand. Arthur's bewildered eyes as he descended into the night.

Vincent was putting the pieces together, too. "And it made Officer Reed shoot himself."

Stef gasped, tension rising within her like an atomic bomb. "What do we do?"

June stepped closer, gently shoving Lenny away.

"June, stop," Vincent said.

"Come on, we have to get back to the lot. We have to call the police," Stef said, wired with panic.

"There's a phone in the ticket booth," Lenny said.

June crouched beside Officer Reed. The hole in his head gaped like a third eye.

Officer Reed's final moments played through June's head as she took his hand. She couldn't access his thoughts, it was like someone else had them. Instead, she felt the cool metal of the gun. Then, nothing more of him.

But there was something else. She saw into the forest. The big oak tree, tallest in the woods, had collapsed. A hissing steam emerged from it. It furled in the moonlight. Beneath the electric glow of lightning, the creature, far smaller, skittered across the ground. Is that where it had come from?

June had to get to the oak tree.

"You guys go," June said. "I have to check on something first."

"June, no," they argued.

"We have to get help before someone else gets hurt," Ingrid said.

"I can't explain, but there's just something I have to do. I won't go far."

Vincent smoothed his hair around its ears, though the gel-slicked style was ruined with sweat.

"Try to get help," Vincent instructed the others. Then to June, "I'm coming with you."

CHAPTER FIFTEEN

Friday, August 7, 1959
11:39 PM

Sticks split beneath June and Vincent's feet. Every snap startled them both.

Shivers crawled along June's spine. Something was on her. She shot a hand over her shoulder and to the back of her neck. She felt only her own skin. No creepy crawler.

"I feel like it's on me," June said.

"I know. That thing could be anywhere in here," Vincent said.

June stopped and listened for any sign of the creature, its spindly legs fighting the mud, or the *click, click* of its snapping pincers.

Haunted string music struck the speakers in the lot. June held a hand to her heart, startled. Laughter ensued. How unnerving it was to hear laughter with three people dead.

She pressed on. The moonlight guided her through the woods, creating shadows of every leaf and every tree. Then, there it was. Split through the middle. The thick trunk lay like a giant brought down by winding rope at its feet.

There was blood on the tree. She saw that first.

Then, as the clouds swayed past the moon, the forest floor illuminated, revealing two bodies.

June stepped back and lost her footing in the mud.

She tumbled to the ground.

Just like that, two more found dead.

She hoped her friends would reach the police on the telephone.

"Oh my god," she said under her breath. She wanted to throw her hands up and scream like the actors in horror films. Let life cut to black. To the next moment in time.

But she couldn't.

She got up and forced herself to take a closer look.

She'd never seen these men before or couldn't recognize them if she had. Not in their pulverized state. Both of their faces were smashed into oblivion.

With what?

When June approached the bodies, something bumped into her foot. She shrieked, but it was only the head of a flashlight. She took a deep breath, preparing herself for a *better view* of the carnage, and flicked the light on.

She listened once more for any hint of the creature nearby but only heard the rustling leaves above and faint fanfare from the lot.

She shooed nasty black beetles away and took the hand of the guy who wore denim jeans, cuffed at the ankles like the greasers did. She thought of the unfurling steam she'd seen when she imagined this tree before.

This guy had died afraid, very afraid. In fact, June had trouble seeing past his fear. It was a red cloud of turmoil. There was shock in it. Disbelief. Betrayal.

Then, pleading.

Who was he pleading with?

Steam furled around June, and the guy stood before her. Injuries gone.

He crouched beside the tree and spoke to someone nearby.

Something sent him toppling over. When he righted himself and came to his feet, June's hand caught his shoulder. She dug her fingers into him as he squealed in pain. The man fell to his knees, whimpering.

"Jim, what are you doing?"

"Jim, let go."

She grabbed a fistful of his hair and slammed his face into the fallen tree. As he wailed, June brought his head back and down again.

A phantom pain pounded into her nose. She tasted blood on her tongue.

But worst of all, she'd felt pride in what she'd just done.

No, not her.

The killer.

The creature.

The pride was its own.

She lowered herself to the tree then. Tears in her eyes.

She braced herself with hands not her own. She reeled her head back and—

Just before she swung it forward, hands caught the sides of her face from behind her and shoved her someplace else.

Bam. Bam.

The bang of a gavel.

Bam. Bam.

June stood ahead of a room full of people. But they were not of this age. They looked more like Puritans. Women wore bonnets and homemade linen dresses, with aprons tied on top. They scowled at her.

"Nancy Jackson, why do you harm these children?" an angry man demanded. She faced ahead and realized the man spoke to her.

Children from behind her squealed. "It's her! She's the witch!"

Bam. Bam.

"This court asks once more of you, Nancy Jackson: Why do you harm these children?"

"I do not, Your Honor."

This voice did not belong to June, though it came from where she stood.

"How do you answer for the children's strange behavior?"

Men and children spat rapid prayers around the meeting house.

"I cannot, Magistrate Cordier."

"It was her!" a child yelled. Seconds later, she began to convulse. A woman pulled the child into her chest, spitting sharp-edged, desperate coos.

The girl thrashed, gurgling and unresponsive.

"Damn you," she said to June. "Damn you, Nancy Jackson! Witch!"

A plump man stood from his seat. Sweat darkened the pits of his button-up. He had a sly smirk about him that June knew she'd seen before.

Bam. Bam.

"Our Heavenly Father who art in heaven," he said, "free us of this evil that has forsaken our children of Your holiness."

Another child fell to the floor. Sputtering on their back and growling.

"Magistrate Cordier, I do not harm these children. I do not make them behave so."

The townspeople shouted their disapproval.

The woman who stood there, as one with June, spoke louder, with greater conviction.

"These children are not ill. God has not left them, though He judges them now for their impishness."

The children exclaimed denial, even the one on the floor growling just moments before. Even the child who had thrashed violently. They all broke through whatever ailed them long enough to defend themselves.

This is mad, June thought.

Hysteria was not a frantic woman like Nora in *House On Haunted Hill* shrieking about a human head in her suitcase. That was valid. Hysteria was not a woman urging others to see the danger she does in men like Professor Jarod in *House of Wax*. Hysteria was not real-world women in doctor's offices demanding answers and better treatment. It's not women reporting to the police, feverishly fighting for someone to believe them. This was all valid.

What was before her, the jeering townspeople. The hatred for this woman. The way they screamed about her without any evidence of wrongdoing. That was hysteria. These people pointing fingers, crossing their hearts and murmuring prayers.

These people were hysterical.

And the woman, no matter how smart or innocent, had no defense that would appease them, nor their fibbing children.

She knew this. June sensed the disappointment, the fear. It made her shudder. She wanted to scream, to kick out of this body, this memory. She knew what was to come.

"Nancy Jackson, for your wicked crimes, I sentence you to death. Do you understand?"

"Please, Magistrate Cordier."

"Do you understand?" the magistrate repeated.

The woman sobbed as accusing eyes glared at her.

"I do," she wept.

Wait, June thought. But she flew away, spiraling back to herself and into someone's arms. She was so dizzy from what she'd seen. She groaned.

"It's me," the voice said.

Her eyes fluttered open.

Vincent.

"What happened?" he asked.

"I saw," June managed through heavy gasps. And then, "I don't understand how people could do that to one another."

"June, what's going on?" Vincent said. "What did you see?"

She caught her breath.

"The creature came from here," she began. "I saw it born from the tree, in steam, then became that thing we saw."

She heard its clicking pincers, and saw them directed at her. She didn't think she'd shake that image.

"Then, it found these two," June motioned to the bodies. "It used that one . . ." She pointed to one guy. ". . . to kill that one," she said, pointing to the man with cuffed jeans. "Then it made him kill himself."

"Like it did with William," Vincent concluded. "But why? What does it want?"

June shook her head, biting her lip.

Then it came to her.

The answer was right there. In the way the kids and adults acted in the meeting house.

A word returned to her. One that she'd heard thrown at women her whole life. At school, at home, and in the pictures, too.

Hysteria.

That's what the creature wanted. Through the one man who killed his own friend, then himself, and through William, Arthur, and Officer Reed, the creature was putting on a show of its own. And to achieve total and complete hysteria, it needed an audience.

Zzzzzzzz.

"What the hell?" June said.

Something moved within the treetops. It shot over the screen, through leaves. The thing was fast and almost neon with its bright white color in the dark. June chased the sound but she didn't have to go far.

The air hurried from her lungs. She gasped.

She feared it was another one of the creature's victims, but it was a gag.

A gimmick.

A skeleton attached to a line zipped over the audience and into the woods.

Like William Castle engineered for theatre audiences seeing *House on Haunted Hill.*

Emergo!

Saturday, August 8, 1959
12:03 AM

As she and Vincent made their way back and away from the hanging skeleton prop, June spotted their friends.

"Were you able to reach anyone?"

"We did," Lenny said.

"But they thought it was a joke!" Ingrid shouted in frustration, tossing her hands up.

"They agreed to send someone out, but it'll be too late by then," Stef said.

"Then we have to warn everyone."

They returned to the lot, panting. The screen was a strange bright white. Hints of blue tinted the edges. June knew that meant that there was no film in the reel. Usually the film switch was quick, precise enough to go mostly unnoticed by the audience.

A cackling menace came over the lot speakers. "From us here at Peterson's Pictures' Dusk Til Dawn Spooktacular, we bring you another treat from the mischievous mastermind William Castle."

Moviegoers talked among themselves, giddy with sugar rushes and at the delicious prospect of being scared to death.

"Ladies and gentlemen, the film you are about to see is maniacal, criminal, and murderous."

The crowd *ooo*ed.

"You'll venture into a morgue, witness body-snatching and the snap-quick descent of the bloody guillotine!"

A recorded scream, a woman. Another joined her. Then another.

"So, we introduce to you, The Fright Break!"

The audience cheered.

"Hurry," June said. "Tell everyone you can."

"Now, now," the showman teased, "we understand some of you might be just *too terrified* to go on. So, we offer you the chance to leave the drive-in theatre now."

The audience booed.

"You may leave the drive-in now," the man said over the speakers. "Go, if you want. Now's your chance. The reel is empty."

A clatter came from the projector, signaling so.

"Take the coward's corner, as Mr. Castle calls it."

June and her friends hurried beside vehicles, hanging on windows, shouting the same warnings. "Get out of here!"

"There's a killer!"

"Go, as fast as you can!

Dread dwelled within June as she and the gang weaved through the rows of speedsters, hot rods, and rust buckets. The creature was still out there. And it could be anyone.

"Please," June said into a truck. "Listen to us, you have to leave."

A math teacher June recognized from school but never had herself waved her off. "I ain't no coward."

He grabbed his swollen stomach as he laughed.

"Just remember to unclip the speakers from your window before pulling away. And for those of you braving the rest of the show, those who think they can survive until dawn, just look at those folks in the coward's corner."

No one was leaving the lot.

Vincent pounded on a closed car window nearby. "Go! Go! Go!"

He smacked the side of the vehicle like a horse out of hell, hoping to startle the driver into action. He'd only awoken a pre-teen's angry grandpa, who gave him a pitiful grin. *Sure, I'll play along,* it said.

"Please, listen to us," Vincent urged. "Go!"

People shook their heads at them. A couple sat on the trunk of their speedster, car top down, pointed and laughed.

"Please, it isn't safe!" Ingrid tried.

No one listened to them. To the audience, they were just part of another gimmick.

"Everyone, go!" Vincent shouted in an explosion of panic.

Hearts pounding, faces red from shouting, the group was exhausted.

"This is real!" Stef stomped. Then, hopelessly, "Why aren't they listening to us?"

People applauded June and her friends, as if they had delivered some kind of performance.

"No takers?" the showman teased over the speakers. "Well, it's your funeral."

The audience laughed.

"Get back to the car," June said.

They tore through the mud, slipping more than a few times. The audience erupted. To them, June and her friends were the fleeting cowards the showman spoke of. And if William Castle encouraged laughter, demanded screams, which he did for these kinds of gimmicks, audiences were thrilled to oblige.

Fear gripped June tight. She sensed the shock. Defeat. Loss of control. Everything the creature needed to turn a person into a killing machine.

It had already found someone. She sensed a disturbance. It scorched her to her core. And this person understood the parasite's goals and that people would die, though they could do nothing to stop it.

She knew the feeling.

But where was it coming from?

Her eyes frantically searched over the vehicles, as she asked herself: Who was man and who was monster?

The answer was almost too terrifying to know. But as far as she could tell, she was the only one who could see it.

And there it was. Razors like little daggers dug into the back of her neck. She raised a hand to the spot, checking for blood. Nothing. The pain wasn't her own.

The creature.

"It has someone else!" June yelled to her friends.

They looked around the lot and back to her. "Where?"

She didn't know yet. Moments passed and the screen crackled with cigarette burn-like dots. It was the changeover cue. That detail nagged at her. The showman was done with his spiel, yet the film hadn't been reloaded.

June awaited more theatrics, *two floating skeletons this time,* another gimmick at play, but none came. She looked to the cement building and the tiny window above concessions, where the projection emitted from.

The screen remained unchanged. *Why haven't they rolled the film?* The projectionist had done it with precision and little disruption that night, so why the delay now?

It hit her, then.

Because he hadn't been there to reload the film.

"It's the projectionist," she said. Then again, shouting to her friends, "It's the projectionist!"

They hadn't known what he looked like, but someone else did.

The math teacher, still believing this was all part of an interactive show, pointed to a man rushing through the lot. "There's the projectionist now!"

The slender man in suspenders ran to the full-bellied teacher who'd pointed him out. He wrapped an arm around his neck, and with the other hand swept a utility blade used for manual film trimming across his neck. Blood jetted from the wound. The injured man instinctively brought a hand to his throat as if that could make it go away, make it make sense, or even slow the bleeding.

June felt a ring of fire around her own throat, a burning phantom pain.

Patrons screamed shrill shrieks of terror, and June was overwhelmed by their fear surging through her. This wasn't like the wandering psychiatric patients or the flying skeleton. This was murder right before their eyes. Senseless and cruel. And it terrified them far more than any horror film ever had. Horror films didn't go that far.

The projectionist then shoved the dull blade through his own eye, securing it in deeply by smacking his palm against it in jellied-wet squelches. Blood seeped from it fast. The man quivered, alive but incoherent, and crumpled to his knees.

For anyone who had questioned whether this was real or simply a gimmick taken too far, this was the indisputable proof. This wasn't *Percepto! Emergo!* Or part of *The Fright Break!*

This was real. There was a monster among them!

"No!" June begged it, wincing, as if her own eye had just eaten a razor blade.

Engines roared to life. Headlights beamed over the lot. Teens leapt into truck beds, calling for the driver to "Step on it!" and "Get us the hell out of here!"

The creature fell from the man. June's eyes zipped through the mud, just spotting it as it hurried to a woman in the convertible Chevrolet Corvair in the next space over. The creature had become even quicker than it had been when it fled from Officer Reed and into the woods.

June brought her hands to the sides of her head. Everyone's fear was so loud. She was like a signal station receiving input from every channel all at once, different voices, commentary, and music streaming into one place. It was information overload.

Two frightened children squealed in the backseat of the Corvair as their mother reached back, wearing a devilish grin. In a swift, single motion, she snapped the younger boy's neck.

The break came with a sickening, crackling pop. The woman sobbed as she lurched for the second boy. She hesitated, fighting her own movements. But the creature had her. And it was fast.

"Help!" The older boy cried.

The woman grabbed the boy's chin and head in her hands, and he was silenced with an identical *pop* as before.

June imagined that this was what an atomic attack would be like. So much death coming at you from every angle. No one is safe. Not even mothers and their children.

The woman then put her Corvair into drive and soared out of her spot, her children's lifeless bodies bouncing around in the backseat. The speaker was still attached to her window, and it ripped from its post in an explosion of glass. Mud sprayed from beneath her tires. She didn't make it far off the lot. Just off to the path.

Then, the woman parked her car at an angle, blocking the exit.

A big, thundering truck dwelled in a sludge of thick mud, its tires only sinking deeper. The driver beat against the steering wheel. "Come on, dammit!"

When it finally left the sloped parking spot, he sped off further than he meant, reaming his truck into the Nash Rambler ahead of it.

June spun around. She'd lost the woman in the Corvair. The creature, too.

"Get to the car!" June ordered her friends. They hurried away, though Vincent and Ingrid lingered a beat longer.

"Go!" June demanded.

Then, June saw a concession worker, the uninterested kid who'd helped her and Vincent earlier that night. He straddled a teen, a friend of Annie's, and struck her again and again with the metal popcorn scoop. Gore flung from her as he shoved the metal into her face and scooped out flesh. Her legs kicked wildly beneath him, like she'd been electrically shocked.

Moviegoers ran around June, fumbling, and crying, panicked and trapped as cars piled into the Corvair with a jarring crunch of metal against metal.

A woman fell in the mud, only to be stomped to death by the massive truck driver. She only screamed once or twice, but the people around her couldn't stop as they watched the behemoth of a man kill with such brutality.

As if in a noir film, a petite blonde woman dug into her purse and pointed a small-frame revolver. However, unlike in the pictures, she didn't miss a beat. She fired and then fired again. The truck driver fell beside the woman he'd just killed, bleeding holes in his chest. The creature struggled out from beneath him, and the woman fired at the ground. It was fast, out of range, and she was out of ammo.

She clicked the trigger, checking once more. She nearly folded in half, and June felt the immense pain of the creature climbing a spine.

She ran to the woman, who raised the gun to her temple, trembling.

But she was too late. She tackled the woman to the ground just as she'd pulled the trigger. *Wait a minute*, June thought.

The woman pressed the trigger again and again.

Click. Click. Click.

No bullet came from its two-inch barrel.

"Help," the woman said, just as she swung the pistol at June.

It barely missed her. Vincent had her by the arm and pulled her away just in time. But they slipped in the mud, not making it far, and she whipped the weapon at June again, this time colliding with the side of her face.

For a moment, she saw stars. Then red smoke.

And then:

Bam.

Bam.

She was back at the meeting house.

"Nancy Jackson, for your wicked crimes, I sentence you to death. Do you understand?"

It was Magistrate Cordier. The death sentence she'd heard delivered before.

And then she was back at the oak tree in the woods, but it stood towering, jutting into the sky like an accusation at God. And she watched as it shrunk, like a time lapse in reverse, over decades, centuries even, the limbs contracting and the trunk twisting in on itself as it shrunk and corkscrewed into the ground. As its sprout disappeared into the soil, the ground fell away into a deep hole. Townspeople stood around it, dancing, cheering, waving torches. And in its depths, June saw severed chicken heads under a swirling mass of crawling beetles. Then a rough-hewn casket was carried over it, horrific screams escaping from its cracks, and June watched it plummet into the hole.

"June!"

Strong hands gripped her face, shaking her.

"June, snap out of it!"

But June understood then. The creature and the woman were one in the same. Whether it knew it or not. And it wanted vengeance. It wanted chaos. Carnage.

Hysteria.

And it got it as the creature hopped from one person to the next, with horrific murder in between.

The screams across the lot were like a standing ovation.

But they hadn't reached the finale, and June knew it wasn't done yet. Vincent brought her to her feet, but she hadn't quite come to. Her body crashed into the ground, and when she finally opened her eyes, she saw a paneled van mow down the blonde nurse she'd seen earlier that night. The woman disappeared under the vehicle. June turned away as it flew by.

She held her breath. She couldn't look.

"She's moving," Vincent said. "June, look."

The woman opened her eyes. Just peeking at the result of what had just happened. She'd lived.

June scrambled over to her. She searched for any injuries. Her eyes went to the blood on her uniform, and the nurse said, "It's not mine."

"Good," June said. "We have to move. Can you walk?"

June, Vincent, and the nurse hurried to their car as the van turned on its wheels and into a crowd of frenzied moviegoers. Their bodies rolling beneath the wheels sounded like the tree limb Ingrid had hopped over on their way to the drive-in.

"No, it's her!" A fifty-something woman pointed at a scrunched-face teen girl with glasses. "She's the killer!"

"Don't accuse my daughter," a woman in a muddied button-up collared dress spat.

June grabbed the nurse's hand and dragged her along as they dodged the mania.

Engines burst as vehicles continued to collide into one another.

Guns fired, and the screams never ended.

When a few drivers hopped from their vehicles and hurried into the woods, the hearse's headlights blared to life. It screeched as it peeled from its spot and over each and every one of them who tried to leave. Heads and limbs rolled between the tires and wheel wells.

All along the treeline, beneath the projector, was mushy brains, meaty piles of blood, and splinters of jutting bones. It was perfectly showcased in the glow of the screen.

With Ingrid already inside, June dove into the Studebaker. The nurse and Vincent hurried in behind them.

Lenny sat in the driver's seat of Vincent's truck. Stef beside him.

Stef and Lenny unclipped their speaker and rolled up their windows. Ingrid hadn't thought of it.

June unclipped the speaker and let it fall. She cranked her window closed as fast as she could.

"June, what's happening?" Ingrid said, distracting June before she could tell her friend to close the window on her side. "I know you know."

Vincent nodded. "She does."

"You do?" the nurse asked.

June felt an aching responsibility and dread with their questions.

"June?" Ingrid tried.

June threw her hands up. "Everyone, stop. I don't know exactly what's happening."

She stopped. Took a deep breath and lowered her voice. "I only know what I saw."

They all self-soothed, rocking their bodies or hugging themselves or bouncing their knees as June began to fill them in on the two found dead in the woods, the meeting house, and the creature born in steam. The open grave and the towering oak. All of it.

Before they could get too far into it, June saw something behind Ingrid.

"Ingrid, look out!" June cried.

The creature was climbing the side of the Studebaker, heading for the crack in the window.

"Close it!" Vincent shouted.

Ingrid pressed on it with both hands, but the crank spun once, twice, and then wouldn't give.

"Close it!" they all chanted.

"I'm trying! It sticks!"

The creature's pincers pointed into the car and down at Ingrid's face, clicking inches away from her nose.

Saturday, August 8, 1959
1:13 AM

June threw the passenger side door open and yanked Ingrid away just before the pincers snapped shut. The creature fell into the seat as the others bolted out and slammed the door shut behind them. The creature hurried across the front bench and crawled up the passenger side door.

Vincent and June stood facing the car with the others. They spread their arms at their sides in protective stances.

The creature wriggled, serpentine-like, up the window. Its legs skittered against the glass. June was relieved. Thankful that she'd closed her window. It's only way out was back the way it came.

"What is that thing?" the nurse shouted.

Lenny turned the key over and over in the ignition. Vincent's truck stalled. He tried a few more times and then the battery died. He gave up and climbed out, Stef behind him.

"We can't leave," Lenny said. "We have to get somewhere safe while we can."

Ingrid had her arms crossed, hugging herself, like she was cold. "Safe? Look what's happened."

The Dusk Til Dawn Spooktacular wouldn't be remembered for its gimmicks or the pictures on screen. It would be remembered in nightmares and flashbacks. In blood. And death.

Violent shrieks circled the lot. People called for their spouses and friends to no avail, some having watched helplessly as their loved ones died. Or killed. Or both.

Green vomit bags blew in the wind and out drivers' windows. Soiled popcorn left random trails in the mud. Bodies, and parts, spread like bloody confetti around the lot. Nearby a person lay face down, the center of her head smushed flat. Someone had driven right over her. The shiny silver of a candy bar wrapper poked out from beneath her dead hand.

The Corvair woman was alive and weeping over her dead children. The creature had left her with the realization of what she'd done. She violently threw her body as she coughed sobs and strained screams.

"Help," she said over and over. "Someone help."

June hoped with everything she had that the police would come soon. How they'd beat the creature, she had no clue. But they'd bring order of some kind. And the remaining moviegoers and police would figure out how to take this thing down, send it back to Hell or freeze it out just like they did in *The Blob*.

Just then, a speedster flew at the Corvair woman. It struck her and pinned her broken body between the two vehicles. The speed nearly split her in two, cutting her off at the bloody rim around her waist.

June had a gut punching pain.

The man shouted from behind the wheel. "Oh my god! What have I done?"

Before the driver could get out, his engine caught fire. The force of the flames shot into the windshield. He screamed only for a few moments. But to June, it repeated. Again and again.

More cars hurried to the exit. Several spun out and crashed into what became a fiery brocade.

Through all of that, June felt the fury of the creature as it climbed around inside Ingrid's car. It would make it back to the other side soon. It was prepared to freefall out the window. Vulnerable for a beat, free to kill again.

"The actors put their stuff in a storage room around back," the nurse shouted, waving them along. "We can barricade the door until the police get here."

Without a better idea, June and the others followed the gimmick nurse behind the concession stand. She found the backdoor marked **STAFF ONLY** and said, "We were supposed to keep this light on."

The nurse felt for the switch and flicked it up and down, up and down. The room sat in disquieting darkness. She grunted and stomped. "Ugh. Let me find the flashlights." Metal and plastic clattered as she felt through the shelves of utility supplies.

The yellow beam of the flashlight clicked on and went out. The nurse beat the thing into the palm of her hand. It flicked on and off. And on again.

Various walls and shelves were lined with chemicals, rod-shaped bulbs, and other supplies labeled with bold red letters: **DANGER**. The nurse pointed the light out before her. It reflected wetness on the floor. Spotted. Smeared. And spattered. Blood of two victims of grotesquerie. The china doll nurse and the man she'd miraculously dragged through the lot.

Projection rods jutted from the man's eye sockets. The eyes themselves were obliterated to bloody sludge. They'd been shoved in so deeply. It would take immense strength to do something like that.

"Betty!" The nurse cried, rushing to the china doll nurse.

Betty wore a necklace of bruises. The nurse tried to bring Betty's head onto her lap but only stretched sticky pieces of skin from the floor, smacking as it tore away. She screamed, absolutely horrified as her friend came apart in her hands.

Lenny held his stomach and gagged. He apologized profusely between breaths.

"Did William do this?" Ingrid said, snapping her neck to look at June. A look that was both afraid and authoritative and said, *Cut the crap and tell me.*

June hadn't quite made it there yet. She cupped a hand over her mouth. Still in shock. But then she remembered the last thing she'd said to William: "*What's that all over your shirt?*"

This is where the blood had come from.

The nurse sobbed. She wiped her dripping nose and sniffled. "Who's William?"

June had to tell them all what she knew if they hoped to survive.

"Yes," June finally said. "William did this." Then she glanced at the man with the rods rammed through his eyes. "But I'm not sure he did that."

The nurse didn't understand. She shook her head, the overwhelm unnerving her like a noir actor does a "*hysterical*" woman.

June turned to the nurse, "What's your name?"

The woman shuddered. "Cathy."

"Cathy," June said. "Was Betty supposed to do that bit tonight?" June pointed to the dead man. "With him?"

June already knew the answer. The strength required for the task of dragging him through the mud was too great for this woman. She'd pulled it off because the creature wanted her to. Because the creature had the power. The audience applauded, cheered, and laughed as the woman dragged away one of the first victims of the night. A horrid creature attached to her spine.

"No," Cathy said.

Vincent pushed through the group, eager to barricade the door. He shoved a work bench beneath the door knob.

Cathy faced June. Still lost and utterly traumatized like the rest of them.

"What's happening, June?" Stef said.

June wasn't sure where to begin.

"I can see things," June explained. "I have these episodes."

The gang nodded along, all having been witnesses to her episodes through the years.

"We know," Stef said.

"No, it's more than that." June shook her head. How could she make them understand?

"She can see dead people," Vincent said matter-of-factly.

Cathy's mouth fell open. Whether she was shocked by the truth or in awe of the insanity wasn't clear.

Ingrid shook her head. "That's not quite it. I saw her . . . She had an episode on Monday morning just before . . ."

June remembered running the track, their exchange with Annie, the cheerleader Janice's broken ankle, and then the intruder.

"Before my grandmother died," June said, "I saw her last moments." She winced at the memory. "And felt the pain of her injuries as she received them. I watched her die."

She'd spoken aloud things she never had before. There was relief in this, but it was too soon to be savored. The screams outside their hideout hadn't stopped.

"It explains so much," Ingrid said. "The headaches. The way you zone out."

June continued. "Yeah, and there's something else. I can see through the killer's eyes."

They all perked up at this.

"What does that mean?" Stef asked, pointing her flashlight away from the bodies on the floor.

"It means that I can see who the creature latches onto next. I can find the next killer."

June watched the group exchange glances.

"If you could see all of that, why haven't you stopped it?" Cathy groaned. Fresh tears welled in her eyes.

That stung, but June understood. She'd been frustrated by the timing of the visions and pain, too.

"This is my first time wandering into it. My *sense,* I mean. That's what I call it. I've never leaned into it so fully. It's scary and painful and sometimes, it's hard to come back. And other times, it's just a cold, vast nothingness that I can't shake for days."

"But Ingrid, you and Vincent have already brought me back. It's something in your touch. In your energy."

She turned to Ingrid. "You did it in the bathroom." Then to Vincent, "And you in the woods." She took a deep breath. "We don't have much time, but I think it's up to us now."

Lenny's eyes widened, and Stef's mouth hung open.

"Have you gone nutty?" Stef asked. "You saw it out there."

Vincent and Ingird understood, though they were just as afraid. June could see it on their faces and sense it in her heart. But she sensed their belief in her, too. She just had to get the others on board. She needed all of their help.

"Stef, as far as I know I'm the only one who can sense this thing. And see through its eyes."

Stef cried and nodded, accepting what she knew to be right. They had to do something. They couldn't just stand there and let more people die. Come dawn, there'd be no one left.

"Where did it come from?" Lenny asked. "It doesn't matter."

"It does. It came from the old oak tree behind the projectors," June said. "Right after lightning struck it down."

Vincent stopped and met her eyes. "What else did you see in the woods?"

"A woman buried alive hundreds of years ago. The whole town accused her of being a witch, and they . . . They just wouldn't listen to reason. She begged them, but they . . ." June shook her head at the memory of raw hatred in the townspeople's eyes.

June turned to Ingrid, "I first saw her when we were in the bathroom earlier. I think she *is* the creature."

This stunned the group.

"What does it want?" Lenny asked.

June answered, staring ahead. "Revenge."

Stef shielded her eyes from the bodies when Vincent's flashlight found them.

"That's it," Vincent cried. "We've got to trap this thing."

"Vincent," Stef whimpered. "Move your light."

He hadn't noticed his beam migrate to the dead man's face, the one they'd all been trying to ignore.

Frightened, Vincent stepped back and stumbled into the shelves on the wall. Bulbs crashed to the floor and shattered around them. Tubs of cleaning solution tumbled and spilled, running red once it met the blood. The image was enough to carry June away into the red clouds of the sense.

"June," someone said.

She shrugged them off. The only way she'd learned anything about the creature was letting the sense take her. And they needed to know more.

"Give me a few minutes and bring me back."

"How?" they asked, but something else caught June's attention. Shadows ran through the red. There and then gone, just like that. She smelled smoke. And there it was, that pleading inner voice of whichever person the parasite had made its own.

Please, let me go.

Where are you, June thought.

But the red clouds fell to infinite black and the question was repeated back to June.

"Where are you?"

She recognized this voice. It was Nancy Jackson.

June didn't answer. She felt a buzzing in her head. The sense vibrating like *Percepto!*

She leaned into and away from Nancy Jackson's echoing, whispered question, "Where are you?"

June summoned what she'd seen at the oak tree: the men mangled beyond recognition, Nancy Jackson and the hysteria of her unjust trial, the children writhing on the floor, the sobbing mothers and shouting men. Then, the moment when the creature detached from Officer Reed as the bullet exited his skull. How it struggled on its back.

It had killed dozens of people by now. But June understood then, like all monsters in the pictures, CO2 in *The Blob* and a wooden stake to the heart in *Dracula*, the creature had a weakness. A vulnerability. And therefore, it could be destroyed. Monsters were always undefeatable, until they weren't. She felt more in control moving through the sense than she ever had before.

"Witch's souls are weightless. Gravity might destroy the body, but the witch's power would remain," the townspeople whispered outside the meeting.

Other theories argued the opposite.

Magistrate Cordier would have the final say, but he heard all propositions, inquiries, and concerns.

"Burn the witch!" children yelled, gleefully. Angry men echoed their chants behind them. "Burn the witch!"

Even still, the children had fooled them all, Nancy thought. And if there was a Devil, he certainly wasn't playing on her side. No one was.

Nancy sat in the meeting house, shackled, as the townspeople came and went. She had brief breaks outside to relieve herself and a few hours of rest following the conclusion of the day's final meeting.

In this final meeting, the priest's wife suggested that Magistrate Cordier order Nancy Jackson to be killed with the help of her strong horses. She said to ensure the witch's death, they would tie each of Nancy's arms and legs to a horse and then let them take off in opposite directions, tearing her wicked body limb from limb.

The barbarity of this execution stunned Nancy silent.

How could she?

Nancy awaited a reaction from the magistrate. He had to think this woman was mad, too. But he didn't denounce her. Didn't deny this cruel and unusual punishment. He simply thanked the woman for the suggestion and sent her on her way, promising to see her at Sunday service.

A mother of one of the allegedly devil-altered children stormed inside the meeting house just as Magistrate Cordier backed away from the podium.

She did not wait for the magistrate to resettle. Intent and fury burned in her eyes. "Magistrate Cordier, hear my declaration. The witch," she said, pointing a bony finger at Nancy, "should not be hanged nor torn apart."

Nancy couldn't take any more of this. What means of execution hadn't they proposed?

"What would you have us do?" the magistrate asked. His tone was far too juvenile and inquisitive for Nancy's liking. In those final days, she watched any decency that remained within the magistrate, lawmakers, and the Christian townspeople go up in flames.

The woman smiled.

"Nancy Jackson terrified those children with her witchcraft. I want her to die *afraid*."

"I did not harm the children!" Nancy shouted, fervently. Silence was getting her nowhere. "Please!"

Nancy hurried forward, stopped by the short lead of metal shackled around her hands and feet.

Her eyes burned with tears. "Magistrate, please! I have not harmed these children. I have not harmed a soul!"

Magistrate Cordier cleared his throat and raised a hand. A man tasked with Nancy's detainment shoved an elbow into her back. Nancy crumpled to her knees, whimpering.

Magistrate Cordier returned his attention to the vengeful mother. "Explain," he said to her.

The woman approached the Magistrate and together, they plotted in whispers. Her eyes never left Nancy as she spoke. And staring her down with trembling fear, Nancy knew this woman, in whatever horrific manner she'd conjured, would seal her fate.

That evening, Magistrate Cordier led the townspeople away from their main roads. Lit torches spotted the dark fields with burning sparks of orange and yellow as they made for the plot of oak trees. The men in the back of the mob lugged a shabby box of oak over their heads. The carpentry of it was heinous, with rigid cracks along its nailed-shut lid and at its sides. But its shape was distinct enough to identify when they'd forced Nancy before it and then inside.

It was a coffin.

Light flitted inside through a small hole in the oak just inches from her face. She pounded her fists against the lid. "Let me out!"

She kicked against the wood at her feet, slamming her heels into it. If she had another thirty or so pounds on her, she might've been able to kick her way out. But she was petite and lethargic, having been fed just enough to keep her alive for the execution.

Still, Nancy fought. She'd known these people all her life. They had to listen. They had to stop this insanity.

"Please! I am no witch!"

Sticks snapped beneath the boots of the townspeople. They jeered, cursing wickedness, cursing Nancy, and any who may have conspired with her.

The children skipped about, singing, "Burn the witch! Burn the witch!"

"There is no conspiracy and no witch here!" Nancy cried. She hadn't conspired with the Devil and against the children. But the townspeople, her neighbors, the midwives she'd befriended, the farmers she purchased food and supplies from, *they* had all conspired against *her*. Plotted her death with cunning and creative cruelty like she'd never seen before.

"Burn the witch!" the children clapped and skipped.

The torches and the nearby trees threw twisted shadows upon the coffin.

Nancy peered through a crack in the wood and saw a pair of strong hands carrying her to her death. A metal cross hung from between his fingers and beneath his palm. It was the priest.

"Father," Nancy heaved. Her lips shook, and she swallowed hard between each word as she said, "Father, God watches. Your congregation. Your wife. Your children. Don't do this."

"It is God's command," the priest answered, coldly.

The group turned a corner and Nancy peered through the opposite side of the coffin. The torches pointed a spotlight at a gaping hole in the earth. It was a grave, six feet deep, and prepared just for her.

Her screams tore through the woods and burned her throat raw.

"Please, I'm begging you! Believe me!"

She threw her fists into the coffin lid, but the nails held fast. Nancy's thoughts scrambled as panic stormed through her. Heavy sobs erupted from deep within her as she

flashed through the life she'd known before this night, before the sentencing, and before the accusation. She mourned the care she gave to people and their children who would destroy her in the name of God. She had once thought that to love God was to love his creation, his people, *all* of his people. But the townspeople loved God because of the wealth the scripture promised in return for faith, loyalty, and obedience. What they believed they served was no God that Nancy knew. They served a king. A tyrant.

Magistrate Cordier stood before the grave, covering his mouth and nose with a hand. "The chicken heads serve what purpose?"

Nancy's nose wrinkled as a putrid smell wafted up from the grave. .

"They're to attract the death beetles," the vengeful mother said.

This made Nancy squeal. The beetles feasted on decaying animal flesh. She'd seen them upon poor rodents, gnawing away at their fur, through their skin, and into the innards.

"Ready now," a man said, and the coffin shook as the men holding it adjusted their grips. "Release!"

And Nancy Jackson felt the coffin fall. A wet smack of blood shot inside and around the coffin as it crushed the chicken heads beneath it.

Pain shot up Nancy's spine and stole her breath. And as she gasped, sucking in air, she knew her time had run out. Nancy had no control. No power. No means to protect herself from this evil. She was terrified, just as the vengeful mother wanted.

The crowd cheered.

"No!" Nancy cried.

The townspeople hummed songs and chanted verses, clapping. The insects skittered from beneath the coffin, climbing over it. Their spindly legs teased the openings of the coffin, nauseating Nancy. Their clubbed antennae poked inside as if peering down at her. One skittered inside and across the inside of the lid of the coffin, just over Nancy's stomach.

Nancy jolted in the wooden confinement, her skin crawling like every beetle had already found its way to her skin. Like they too understood death would come and her body would soon be their feast.

Thunk!

A fraction of the light disappeared as a shovelful of dirt poured over her.

Thunk!

The crowd clapped, amused. "Bury the witch!"

How could they make entertainment out of such an atrocity?

Thunk!

Thunk!

Nancy was losing the light. Losing her breath. It rasped weakly within her lungs and held within the swell of her throat.

They had turned their backs on the good and giving nature they preached every Sunday. They'd turned their backs on God. And most devastatingly, they'd turned their backs on her.

An even worse thought occurred to Nancy as dirt beat against the coffin.

God turned his back on me.

What a betrayal. The weight of it hiccuped within her and her body faltered with a sob. Dirt crumbled above her and into the hole of the oak. The grainy texture fell over her face and hands. A shovelful at a time.

She'd lost the light entirely, but she could hear the beetles surrounding her.

This was her worst nightmare.

She thought even Hell would be better. It had to be.

And that gave her an idea. It frightened her, but not as much as the townspeople had, nor as much as God's abandonment of her.

Nancy had one place left to cast her hope.

She summoned images of him. She'd seen them in crude paintings inside the church and children's bible studies. There was the fork-tongued Devil with thick and twisted horns like a black goat's, and the Devil as a shadow, the elusive entity who wore masks of virtue.

She brought her hands over her stomach like how they typically pose the dead, and said, "My King. I call upon you."

Thunk!

Nancy winced.

"Can you feel my fury? Your hellfire burning within me?"

She was running out of time, fast.

God preached love. To preach to Satan, she'd need fury.

"I curse this town and all those who live in it!" She wheezed and began again. "You will all die and the beetles will feast upon you!"

Her eyes felt heavy, her head weightless.

"And all your children to come. And when they do," a maniacal energy stormed through Nancy, igniting her lungs with fury and filling her with conviction, "I will laugh!"

The latter phrase boomed like heavy claps of thunder. Earth shook from the walls of the grave, swallowing the coffin further.

Muffled gasps broke through the crowd above.

"And laugh!" Nancy boomed.

The men worked more quickly.

Thunk!

Thunk!

Then, she prayed. Pleaded, whispering furiously, "Satan, save my soul. Save my soul, and I will serve you."

The air thinned beyond recovery and Nancy mumbled, choking on the words, "Give me vengeance, and I will make them bleed for you."

Then, she closed her eyes and awaited the inevitable.

But moments later, heat exploded from within her heart, into her lungs, her bones.

"Can it be?" Nancy asked.

"You shall have vengeance," came a fierce voice, whispering in her ear. It was otherworldly. Unholy. And so close, she could feel its hot lips on her skin. "And, my dear Nancy, your resurrection shall be glorious."

Nancy screamed a hoarse and silent roar, everything within her on fire.

The coffin shook, sending beetles toppling beside it and others scurrying to the surface and heading for townspeople's feet. They revolted and shrieked.

Then, came a horrifically disturbing bout of laughter. Not from any of them, but from deep within the grave. Perhaps even from beneath it. For the voice they heard was not that of Nancy

Jackson. They'd hear no more cries of agony from her. No more pleading. Only the haunting bellows from the sudden burst of steam and smoke that escaped the buried coffin.

It furled around the villagers, hanging in the air around them. They turned on their heels and huddled together, watching it move about them.

The villagers yanked their children away. And soon, all the townspeople, the vengeful mother and magistrate, too, were sent screaming and running from the trees.

Before June returned to herself, with the help of Ingrid's cooing, June turned from the scene and faced Nancy Jackson, her grey skin crawling with carrion beetles.

A revelation came to her. No pain. No death. June just knew.

"The creature is coming," June said.

And she saw who it wanted.

The sound of clicking pincers grew louder by the second.

She remembered them pointing at her in the woods. And then coming for Ingrid in the car.

But it hadn't been coming for Ingrid.

It was after June.

CHAPTER EIGHTEEN

Saturday, August 8, 1959

1:36 AM

W hen June came to, she pointed her flashlight over the mess of supplies Vincent had sent crashing to the floor. She saw orange and red caution labels:

WARNING!

DANGER!

FLAMMABLE!

And that gave her an idea.

"Vincent's right," she said to the group. "We have to trap this thing. And then we kill it."

Cathy finally came to her feet. "How do you kill that thing?"

June imagined herself in a noir film, or even in *The Tingler*, when Vincent Price's character takes note of all he's learned in his lab and from his experiments. That's what they had to do. Get everything on the table and pick out what would save them. Because they had to make it. All of them had to, June thought.

"What do we know about the creature?" June asked the room.

"We know it makes people kill," Stef muttered.

"And it gives them the strength to do it so . . ." Cathy looked back at Betty once more, choking up. ". . . so viciously."

June nodded. "And we know it doesn't just leave anyone behind for dead. It kills because it wants more than sensation and shock. It wants *hysteria*."

That made the group uneasy. Stef shifted, moving closer to Lenny. Lenny adjusted his letterman sweater, bringing it closer to his neck, wrapping the front around him.

"That's why it hadn't been satisfied with just killing the man Betty dragged around the lot," June continued. "It wanted people to react, even if they didn't realize what they cheered and applauded for. And then, it brought him back here to . . ." June's words fell off. The dead man with rods jutting from his skull hadn't gone anywhere. They all knew what had happened next. ". . . and it knew someone would find it."

June wondered if the creature had known she would discover it.

"So this thing is wicked fast," Ingrid said, "freakishly strong, can make its host kill, and it wants to kill all of us."

Stef groaned. "What are we supposed to do," she said, clearly frustrated and terrified.

June pressed the group. "Come on. What else do we know?"

Lenny bit his bottom lip. His eyes stared ahead like he was somewhere else. "What we saw with Officer Reed. We know that the creature falls from its host once they're dead."

The group was silent with a collective reimagining of that traumatic scene.

"I've been thinking about that, too," June finally said. "How it toppled over onto its back. And the way it looked at me. I don't know what it means. But we do know one more thing.

Something I learned at the healing tree. That creature, that thing hunting us, used to be human.

"Her name was Nancy Jackson. They accused her of witchcraft. And then buried her alive."

The blood drained from their faces.

June nodded. "Yeah."

She let this sink in a minute.

Click.

Click.

June spun around. Ice speared through her veins. The creature's pincers. It was as if she'd summoned it herself, materializing it with the spoken name: *Nancy Jackson.*

"It's here," June said with unnerving certainty

They searched the space with their flashlights, rediscovering the bloodbath on the floor. They'd shared this much time, intimately confined, with two dead bodies. The perversion of it. The savagery.

Dry weeps escaped Cathy's overexerted lungs.

A thundering boom collided with the supply room's door.

"Everyone stay sharp," Vincent said.

Boom.

Boom.

Each hit sent dread drumming through June. She ground her teeth as panic tightened the gang together.

Boom.

Boom.

"How did it find us?" Stef shrieked.

June wondered, did the sense really work both ways? Could that explain what led the creature to them in the Studebaker?

Pain struck June's head like a sudden headache. But it came again and again as the battering ram fired into the door. She pressed her fingers into her temples. She had to fight the drilling aches. She couldn't let the pain carry her away.

Boom.

Boom.

The workbench scooted forward with each *boom*. The door shook in its frame, the hinges whining as they weakened. The door blew open, and the bench crashed into the far wall. June and her friends covered their heads and quickly crouched as debris flew over them.

Somewhere, a cable or pipe ruptured, screaming like a tea kettle as it released steam.

Steam.

The creature was born in steam.

A figure stood against the night, brutish and bloodied. June pointed her light at the man and stifled a scream. Then, she noticed that he held something in his arms. A person. An old man, delirious with pain. His head crumbled at the crown, blood pouring from it. His neck contorted into a sharp bend, head lolled to one shoulder, jammed in place like a puzzle piece that wouldn't fit. The creature had used *him* as the battering ram.

Ingrid bellowed a horrified wail. June could feel her friend's devastation twisting inside of her. It was the pain of knowing she couldn't save him. She'd felt it every time Ingrid's eyes absorbed death.

The creature's host discarded the body with a savage throw.

Ingrid gasped like she'd been gutted.

The old man smacked into the blood pool beside Betty and the man with the rods shoved through his eyes.

June snapped her neck to Cathy. She couldn't focus on Ingrid and get lost in her pain.

"Cathy?" June shouted.

Cathy met June's eyes with a wild terror.

"How do we get to the projection room?"

Cathy's mouth hung open. Her eyes darted from side to side. She was in the throes of trauma.

"Cathy!" June screamed.

The urgency awoke her from her stupor. "It's that way," Cathy said, pointing an unsteady finger just left of where the supply room door had crashed. She hadn't seen it in the shadows until Cathy pointed her flashlight at it.

A strong breeze swirled through the supply room. June smelled smoke, exhaust, and the earthy-metallic stench of blood.

The screams across the lot had grown quieter, more of an echoing whimper with an occasional plea for death.

The creature's host beamed, absolutely glee-ridden with their shock. The stomp of the man's foot shook supplies from their shelves.

"Uhm, June?" Stef squeaked. "What do we do?"

The creature's host stood strangely still then, daring them to move.

June tried to devise a plan. The creature was most vulnerable when it detached from a person, but that person had to die first. She wasn't a killer, even if she was somehow physically capable of overpowering the creature and its host.

June reached for one of the bottles of cleaning solution. The plastic label was riddled with warnings like a William Castle film. She hoped it would do the trick.

"Ingrid, do you still have Arthur's matchbook?"

Ingrid produced the matchbook and tossed it to June.

"When I say so, everyone run," June said.

"What?" Ingrid protested.

"June, no!" Lenny said.

"Just run!" June shot back.

The creature spurred the man forward and he ran at them. June spun the cap free from the jug of the all-purpose cleaner and threw it in his face. This only disoriented him momentarily. She grabbed another jug and ran in the opposite direction of her friends.

"Get out of here!" June hurried for the projection room.

The man lunged after June, and the pair slid in the blood and cleaner. She yelped as the host grabbed her arms, shaking the jug of the hazardous chemicals from her hand. Then, the man was on her.

She fought, trying to worm out from beneath him or at least guide him closer to the busted bulbs. "Get out of here!" June commanded her friends.

The man's strong hands released her only to grab at her throat. She clawed at the hands, but the creature was undeterred. It could kill her with a single snap, like it had so many others. But it wanted to savor her fear. Relish in her friends' anguish.

Vincent rushed the creature's host, but it sensed the attacker. It raised its host to his feet, pinning June down with a thick, muddied boot at the center of her chest, and shot an arm out. Vincent's throat collided into it, and his feet swung out from beneath him. He fell hard against the cement floor, the wind knocked out of him.

As the creature turned, June saw its pincers around the back of the man's neck. It clicked them at her.

Ingrid came from behind them with her arms above her head, a long projection rod in hand, and shattered it over the top of the host's head.

Stef followed up with another, screeching like a warrior as she brought it down.

Lenny brought a rod to his shoulder and got into his baseball stance. He swung the rod right into the front of the man's face like he was smashing a ball out of the park.

The creature's host collapsed beside June.

She rolled away, trying to recover her breath. But there wasn't time. And they all knew what came next.

The creature fell free from its host's spine.

Cathy hurried on top of an overturned milk crate. That gave June an idea.

"Trap it," June croaked. Pointing at Cathy's feet.

Cathy hesitated. Her whole body jolted with fear.

Ingrid put it together. "The crate, Cathy! Trap it with the crate!"

Lenny hurried to her, like he was about to dump her off of it. But before he could, Cathy lept off and wielded the crate, closing the distance before her and the creature. It turned, leaping into the air and clicked its pincers at her. She caught it in the crate and rammed it to the cement ground.

The creature shrieked in a shrill, sharp cry of fury.

There was a moment's pause, before the inevitable. The creature flexed its powerful body, sending Cathy and the crate flying away from it.

"Cathy!" Ingrid called.

"Great, we've pissed it off!" Lenny shouted.

The creature sped its way to Vincent, and before they knew it, it had scurried up his back and latched onto his spine.

"June!" he tried.

And then the creature buried his consciousness. It was in charge.

"Vincent," Ingrid wailed, "are you alright?"

"Don't talk to it," June said, struggling to her feet.

Vincent brought his hands out before his face, turning them over. The creature inspected its new host.

"No, no," Stef wept. "Leave him alone!"

Vincent leapt toward Stef. She ducked, and Vincent collided into Lenny instead. The two wrestled on the floor.

"Grab all the chemicals you can," June said, "and get to the projection room. Dump them everywhere!"

June's friends were frozen with fear.

"Do it!" June commanded.

Ingrid, Cathy, and Stef did as June said and snatched chemicals off the shelf.

"June!" Lenny shouted, just dodging Vincent's fists slamming toward his face and into the floor.

Vincent shoved Lenny aside and raced to a shovel hanging beside a rake and outdoor broom.

"He's going to kill us!" Something broke within Cathy. She ran for the exit, and in doing so, caught the creature's attention. With his free hand, Vincent snatched her by her hair. She yelped.

"Let her go!" Ingrid screamed.

It had her on her back in an instant. Vincent planted one of his thick, muddy work boots onto Cathy's chest.

"No," she sobbed. "No, no."

She writhed beneath him, tugging at Vincent's pant leg, the toe of the boot, trying to get him off. He pressed more weight into her chest. She coughed against it.

"Vincent!" Ingrid repeated his name. Trying to break through the creature's control to no avail.

Vincent was gone, and the creature was ready to make a spectacle of the girl.

It loved a good audience.

Vincent raised the shovel above him and sent the blade down into Cathy's neck. The wet end of the shovel raised once more, and with the creature's tremendous strength, it severed Cathy's head from her body with a gory squelch.

Stef and Ingrid screamed. They'd made it to the door, but needed to get to the projection room. It was just up the stairs.

"Go!" June ordered them, trying to focus and fix her eyes away from the decapitated nurse.

They threw the door open and hurried up the cement steps.

Lenny froze, eyes wide with a shock that struck him greater than anything else that night. He'd just watched his best friend kill a woman. Just after he'd tried to kill him.

"Vincent," June said, "I know you can hear me in there."

Vincent stared her down. He grinned wickedly, dipping his chin just as the china doll nurse, Betty, had done.

"I'm going to get it off you," June promised, tears in her eyes. "I'm going to kill it."

But she wasn't sure how to do both.

And she couldn't let him kill anyone else.

Vincent still held the shovel. He looked at the dripping blade, then at Lenny, and back to June.

Ingrid and Stef had returned.

"It's done, June! Now what?" Ingrid cried.

June felt Vincent's fear as the creature flexed his fingers and tightened them around the shovel handle.

She remembered those moments from her childhood with Vincent; watching scary movies in her basement or those late nights at the drive-in when their mothers believed they were asleep. How he had comforted her at her grandmother's funeral. How he'd called her back from what she'd seen in the woods. And how he had been one of the first people to introduce June to the feeling of being *known* by someone. To have someone who could read you so easily.

"I'm going to get it off you," June repeated, searching the room. She held her hands up, as if to say, *easy now.*

But she felt something else, too.

Resignation? Had the creature already subdued him so completely?

She concentrated. *Vincent,* she said internally, hoping to reach him on some other level.

The silence was excruciating.

Vincent.

Vincent's expression didn't change. This was it. She had to get him away from the others. She had to fight or free him on her own. She backed toward the door to the projection room. Her friends inched closer to the exit.

The creature eyed them both.

Look over here. I'm the one you want, June thought.

Vincent turned toward the others, and he lifted the shovel, ready to run at them.

"Nancy Jackson!" June leapt up and down.

Then, she recalled the magistrate, the trial, the townspeople.

"Why do you harm these children?" June bellowed. And then, "Burn the witch! Burn the witch!"

Vincent hissed, shooting his deathly gaze from June's friends and back to her. She could feel the fury behind the creature's eyes. The vengeance it craved so deeply, so primitively. This is what those people had done to her, and now, Nancy Jackson came to collect the cost.

"Nancy Jackson!" June roared. "Why do you harm these children?"

Vincent growled at her, and Lenny pulled her friends along. June had to keep it up. Keep the creature mad and coming at her.

What had the priest said when Nancy Jackson pleaded with him as they carried her to her grave?

"It is God's command," June cried. There was disbelief within the creature. June could sense the bewilderment. After all this time, this single line from a person Nancy believed to be of great virtue, one that had condemned her on a whole other level, shook the creature.

Vincent hissed. Spit flew from his lips like a wild animal. Or a hysterical townsperson.

"Come and get me!"

"June, no!" Ingrid cried.

Lenny hurried her and Stef along, eventually lifting Ingrid off her feet, and carried her away kicking and screaming.

June backed toward the stairs. Vincent followed, step by step. She had to keep its attention on her to give her friends time to escape.

"Nancy Jackson, for your wicked crimes, I sentence you to death!" she said, echoing the magistrate's verdict.

Vincent hissed in rage and lunged toward her, but then stopped.

Vincent, inches from her own face, dropped the shovel.

June jumped at the sound of clattering metal.

A wicked smile spread over Vincent's face, but June could see the fear deep in his eyes. Could feel the panic rising within her friend.

June swallowed rising sobs. "Fight it, Vincent."

In a quick motion, before she could comprehend what he was doing, Vincent grabbed the side of his face in one hand, and his jaw in the other, and twisted. In a quick *snap*, Vincent was dead.

June screamed like she never had before. A pain beyond pain caught fire in every nerve of her body. She sobbed and grunted, outraged and utterly devastated all at once. And she understood then how revenge had taken over Nancy Jackson so completely. How it had somehow manifested into that monstrous resurrection. She understood that burning desire for vengeance, and she would have hers. She would kill Nancy Jackson.

June still stood at the door. She had Arthur's matchbook in her hand.

The creature slinked to her quickly, growing larger by the second.

June waited just long enough to push the door wide enough for the creature to pass through it.

When it did, she hurried for the stairs.

The creature snipped at her heels.

She struck the match head against the strike surface, and the wood snapped into two.

June hurried for another.

The projection room was full of film reels and canisters, just as June had hoped. It only had one window for projection. June would need to close them to extinguish any oxygen. She couldn't let any steam escape from the room.

The creature crested the final stair, and June dashed to the window and slammed the shutters closed.

Ingrid and Stef had splashed the cleaner onto the small wooden table, and June thought that's where she'd start. She struck another match. When a tiny flame burned at its head, she threw it onto the table, and it was immediately engulfed.

The creature scurried toward her and climbed along her legs. She kicked it from her and it crashed into a pile of film canisters. They toppled over, and film split out of them like innards.

The reels burst into flame, and June pulled down another shelf of canisters into the roaring fire. The blaze was all around her now, and thick black smoke billowed from the inferno. June could feel her skin begin to sear.

The creature scurried for the projection window in an attempt to escape the flames, but the shutters were closed tight. Then, it tried for the door to the stairs, but it too was closed shut and blocked with a thick, black cloud of suffocating smoke.

June felt its panic. It was acrid amongst her senses. Foreign and familiar all at the same time. June had panic of her own, but it wasn't as harsh. She tried to give it space as the flames sparked around her, quickly eating away the room. There was nowhere to go. She already knew that, just as Nancy Jackson had known it once they'd put her in that shabby, oak coffin.

It's over, Nancy, June thought.

The creature erupted in violent, shrill shrieks as the flames found its spindly legs.

Nancy Jackson was never a witch, June knew. But together, they'd burn.

And even if it returned to steam, in that cement room with the window closed, it would still perish.

The creature was afraid then.

The fire reached her feet and traveled over her. The burning pain was fast, an agony beyond agony. But along with the pain, June sensed a quiet peace she hadn't had all week.

And then, she closed her eyes, taking her mind to driving in the Studebaker with Ingrid. Sitting beside the truck as Vincent fiddled underneath it with grease-covered hands. Stef's primping. And Lenny's kindness. Arthur's cool aloofness. Her friends.

She envisioned them all together.

And then, above her, she saw only Ingrid. She cupped June's face and kissed her.

In those final moments, she'd carried herself away to a place less painful than all the others before.

She took a final breath, knowing she'd see her friends again.

Vincent was already waiting for her.

Friday, August 12, 1960
9:30 PM

I ngrid drove the Studebaker along the lone path to Peterson's Pictures with Lenny and Stef sitting beside her. Skeletal limbs of the surrounding oak trees still made for somewhat of an obstacle. Ingrid had revisited the lot so many times, though, that she casually turned the wheel to left and then to the right without missing a beat.

They'd driven by the lot on late nights where they just drove and no one spoke. What happened at the lot had become a sort of phenomenon.

No one believed the story about a monster that could latch onto people and make them kill at will. Not anyone who wasn't there.

They'd wished they'd had better explanations for June's and Vincent's and Arthur's parents. And for their own, because after what they'd seen, what they'd been through, they'd been forever changed. The memories crept into daydreams and dominated their nightmares.

The remainder of their gang made it through the woods that night with cars smoking and gore everywhere they stepped. The police had finally come just as they'd peeled back the last of the brush. Stepping out on the other side felt like stepping away from everything they'd known before that night. Because from then on, everything was different. Everything was sadder, like the world now had a permanent lens of gray even in the most colorful and joyous of moments. It was like that for Ingrid, anyway.

Lenny and Stef had each other.

But Ingrid, she felt more alone than she ever had before. Part of her wished she'd ignored June and stayed with her. Fought harder as Lenny carried her to safety. She wished she was stronger. Half as strong as June.

June was sensitive, as in caring and thoughtful. She had those strange episodes. They seemed awful at times. So jarring and unsettling. And she couldn't imagine the things June had seen the night of the massacre at the drive-in. Maybe if she'd stayed behind and followed June to the projection room, she could've asked her in those final moments. She could have told her what she wanted to say for so long. "You're so brave, June," or "You're so special," or "You're the toughest person I know." Because she didn't think June had heard any of that as often as she should have. It was something the gang all knew of her. Her oddities, though they didn't understand it, not before the DUSK TIL DAWN SPOOKTACULAR, were part of June just as much as her love of horror movies was, or even the bright blonde color of her hair. And carrying something like that, navigating it, and for good, was something truly incredible.

Ingrid pulled the Studebaker up to the entrance of the abandoned drive-in lot, and this time decided to go in. The marquee was unlit, but with the sun still peaking over the horizon, Ingrid saw that it still listed the films from that night. The **T** in the *The Tingler* had fallen away, so it read, *THE INGLER.*

Ingrid appreciated now what the night had meant to June after losing her grandmother. Ingrid smiled. Seeing any of the titles Vincent Price had starred in made her think of June, her horror cinephile.

Lenny and Stef had given up on horror movies.

But Ingrid saw every one released over the past year. She felt like she'd have to tell June all about them one day. The films she'd missed. A *blonde* Vincent Price in a Roger Corman flick released that summer. A Poe adaptation called *House of Usher.* William Castle's latest, *13 Ghosts.* It didn't star Price, but Ingrid knew June would appreciate the fun of it just the same. She would've loved the new Alfred Hitchcock film, too. And she knew June would've been stunned and then absolutely delighted by the fact that they'd cast Janet Leigh just to kill her off so early in the film.

The first time Ingrid went to the theatre alone, she'd had an anticipatory dread that made it tough to sit still. The room felt like it shrank, the walls trapping her.

Then, a blissful warmth wrapped around her like an intimate embrace.

A tear fell from her eye. "June," she'd whispered.

She'd seen *House of Usher* every time it played. And she'd sat through double-features, picking apart horror films, analyzing every scare, shadow, and sound, just as June had done. And in this way, Ingrid felt her friend. She knew she was there.

They pulled into the lot and saw the graveyard that had become of the drive-in lot. Authorities had cleared the cars that blocked the main path into the lot, only so emergency vehicles could get through, but so many others remained. Some were charred down to their frames, others sat upon half-melted rubber tires. Vincent's truck remained in the same spot. His family never sent for it. The town didn't want any relics of that night out and about. In his pocket, Lenny still had the key. They never went inside Vincent's truck, but they took their spot beside it, as if the gang was all here, meeting once again, for another night of horror flicks.

None of the old smells remained. Not the delicious scent of buttery popcorn or burgers on the grill. It smelled of fire and ruin. Gasoline and death.

If Ingrid wasn't careful, the nostalgia would escape her and she'd see only a sea of corpses. Reimagine the projectionist slitting the throat of a math teacher just before shoving the blade into his eye. Or the Corvair woman snapping the necks of her young boys, only for her to be crushed between two vehicles, and lost in an explosion of fire moments later.

When Stef turned her head into Lenny's shoulder, Ingrid grabbed her friend's hand, keeping one on the wheel.

And like that, all the bad evaporated like steam in the air. She remembered June sitting in the front seat with her and Stef. Stef fixing June's hair and Doris Day on the radio. June wouldn't want them to forget Peterson's Pictures Drive-In Theatre. It was her favorite. She loved it so much that she'd come to the DUSK TIL DAWN SPOOKTACULAR at the height of mourning her grandmother's murder.

Lenny unraveled a pack of beignets. The local baker, who had parked beside them that night, survived by tucking himself away, beneath the dash of his vehicle. He'd said he waited out the night. Closed his eyes and tried not to hear all the screams. Ingrid sometimes became angry at this fact and wondered if they had they done the same, maybe her friends, Arthur, Vincent, and June, would still be alive.

But June had a role to play, and she knew it.

Sweet June.

Stef squeezed Ingrid's hand, and Lenny passed both of them a beignet.

"It's sweet that we keep getting boxes of these," Stef said, "but June wouldn't approve." Stef laughed to herself, fighting tears. "She'd say, 'No movie night is complete without a big ol' bucket of popcorn.'"

Lenny laughed. "And she'd finish a family-size bucket all by herself before the first flick was over."

This made Ingrid smile. She remembered Vincent huffing and puffing about June hogging the popcorn.

"I feel her here," Ingrid said, batting away happy tears. "I do so often."

Lenny and Stef exchanged glances.

"What was your favorite film that night?" Ingrid asked her friends, popping the beignet into her mouth. The sweet rush of sugar did in fact feel wrong. Ingrid now agreed that popcorn and movies were the indisputable duo. Popcorn was a must. She'd make some on the stovetop the next time she drove out to Peterson's Pictures.

When they didn't answer, Ingrid said, "I wish we could've seen *House of Wax*. June told me about it. That's the Vincent Price poster she has in her room, too."

Vincent Price and his prized wax figurine of Marie Antoinette.

But they hadn't seen it.

"I've watched it since then. You guys should too," Ingrid encouraged. "I don't know how, the sense, maybe, but I'm telling you, she's still here. And she lives through those films."

Ingrid put three cigarettes between her red lips and lit them all with a single match. She passed one to each friend.

"So, what?" Lenny asked. "You think if we sit out here, she'll talk to us?"

Ingrid wasn't wounded.

She'd questioned it when it happened for her, too.

"How about Vincent or Arthur?" Stef asked. "Do you ever feel them?"

Lenny looked to Ingrid, anticipating her response.

"I haven't," she said. "I don't think it works the same way for them."

This unsettled Stef. She sighed and wiped streaming tears from her face.

"But I don't think sensing June would feel like this if they hadn't gone someplace good. When I sense her," Ingrid said, lips quivering, "I just sense peace."

Lenny shook his head. "But how? How it ended was so unfair."

He balled his hands into fists.

Stef rubbed his shoulder.

"But she saved us," Ingrid said, smoke unfurling from her lips.

He nodded, knowing what that would've meant to June.

"It'll hurt for a long time," Stef said.

"It will," Ingrid agreed. "But the three of us are here to hurt and heal together. And for that, I'm so grateful to our friends."

Ingrid looked into the dark woods, above the projector.

And once more, Ingrid felt a warm embrace envelop her.

Ingrid raised her cigarette to the dark screen and said, "To our friends. To Vincent, Arthur, and June."

Lenny and Stef followed suit, raising the smoking ember ends of their cigarettes to the roof of the Studebaker.

"To our friends," they echoed.

Ingrid swallowed tears and said, "And to all the crazy horror films to come. June would've loved them."

This made Stef smile. "And she would've loved to see them scare the hell out of me."

They laughed and smoked until the cigarettes were almost too small to hold between their fingers.

And when they turned on the radio, they heard an old ghost tale being read with heavy organ music in the background. The voice said, "Good evening. My name is Vincent Price . . ."

Acknowledgements

The Film You Are About To See would not exist without the following people:

First and foremost, Joey Powell and Mad Axe Media. Thank you for believing in women in horror and giving us a safe space to create. Also for pointing out to me that I write period pieces. This was news to me but made me more confident going into a story set in 1959.

To my editor, Clay, who has been with me since writing *Not Another Sarah Halls* back in 2018. Your guidance, friendship, and unshakable faith in me have kept me going. I love our late night chats that always leave me feeling less anxious and more certain of my place in the horror community. This one is really for you.

To Jer, who not only read the horrendous and wildest early versions of this book with patience and an eagerness I'll never understand, but who I appreciate immensely. You kept me fed, happy, and supported me every step of the way. Not to mention, you sat through countless hours of oldies horror movie marathons and listened to my spiels about every one. One of the my proudest moments of creating this story was knowing that I made an oldies horror fan out of you. Thank you for always taking me to celebrate finishing a writing project with books and our veggie cheeseburgers.

To William Castle, Vincent Price, and everyone who has been a part of the gimmick/oldies horror legacy, I thank you for all the fun and inspiration over the years. Not to mention, the comfort in a world that feels more distressing by the second. And thank you to Elvira, Victoria Price, and anyone else who continues to introduce Price and Castle to new audiences. They live on through you.

To my sister, Hanna, who was always there when I needed a pep talk. And thank you for being my first oldies horror movie buddy. I'll never forget that first night when we stumbled on *House On Haunted Hill* and then went down a rabbit hole of Vincent Price movies.

To all the horror authors who inspire me and have offered support and kind words, including Clay McLeod Chapman, Todd Keisling, Nat Cassidy, Sadie Hartmann, Cynthia Pelayo, Josh Malerman (he just said the title of *Take Your Turn, Teddy* was cool, but how could I not mention that?!), Angela Sylvaine, Wendy Dalrymple, Rachel Harrison, Silvia Moreno-Garcia, Isabel Canas, and so many others.

To my spooky friends: Mike Salt, Thomas Gloom, Spencer Hamilton, Briana Morgan, Kyle Winkler, Jeremy Megargee, Mona Kobbani, Michael R. Goodwin, Kelly Brocklehurst, Marcus Hawke, Kalvin Ellis, and Jamie Stewart. Our chats give me life.

And once more to Spencer Hamilton, who has believed in me in times I couldn't find a fraction of belief in myself. I appreciate your friendship more than you could ever know. Cheers to you, my brilliant friend.

To the Books of Horror team and community. I love being a part of this group and discovering so many excellent horror titles that I might have otherwise missed.

To two local, independent bookstores who always keep my work, and the work of so many of my horror friends, stocked on their shelves, Main Street Books and Second Flight Books.

To Flora Candle Co. for making and continuously restocking my favorite "writing" candle when I tore them all from your shelves. A trip to your store is always a great writing break. Please give me Miley Cyrus "Something Beautiful" candles next.

To my childhood friend, Tyson, who ensures that we speak every single day no matter how busy we are. You rooted for me as I wrote, edited, rewrote, and edited this book. Your encouragement means the world.

Lastly, to the readers. It's been awhile since I gave you something new, but I hope *The Film You Are About To See* was worth the wait. Thank you for your continued belief in me. I truly hope to make oldies horror fans out of you all. And if you watch any of the films shared in the book, please share and tag me: @haleynewlin_author

Special shoutout to a superfan, Adam Allen. Your support of indie horror never ceases to amaze me. Thank you, my friend.

About the Author

Haley Newlin grew up watching Vincent Price movies and listening to The Beatles, both of which have heavily influenced her work. She has published two novels previously, and her short fiction is featured in Kandisha Press' SLASH-HER anthology, which has received praise from Stephen Graham Jones and Barbara Crampton. Newlin is also a writer for Cemetery Dance Magazine.